# Across
# Americana

# Across Americana

*A Novel*

Tom Malone

Denver, Colorado · 2016

Library of Congress Control Number: 2016905165
ISBN-13: 978-1-945236-08-2
ISBN-10: 1-945236-08-6

Printed in the United States of America

Second edition, 2018

Published by Malone Media · Denver, Colorado

*To Nikki:*
*For your eternal love and support.*

*"The man who goes alone can start today; but he who travels with another must wait till that other is ready."*

– Henry David Thoreau

*Walden*, 1854

# PROLOGUE

As the spring of 2012 approached, soon-to-be college graduates began to search for their dream jobs. Accounting students scoured their LinkedIn accounts for potential job openings as Certified Public Accountants. Business majors called and emailed every potential contact they made during their tenures in college. Engineering graduating students interviewed at laboratories and factories across the country.

Unfortunately, 2011 saw some of the worst business losses in recent United States history. The U.S. unemployment rate sat steadily near 9 percent; though this statistic had dropped by one percentage point since 2010, the number loomed over the newly-educated who vowed to enter the workforce.

Old marketing and advertising jobs were shapeshifting; the social media boom had reinvented the concepts behind marketing campaigns. The technology revolution, the popularization of the smart phone, and the exponential growth of social media apps created new sectors in nearly every business. In other words, digital media students had it made.

The ones who lost out were the students of traditional journalism. Students who entered college with aspirations to be Bob Woodward and Carl Bernstein had to make other arrangements. Blogs made the citizen journalist a likely replacement for highly-trained reporters and gifted writers. Students of traditional journalism were forced to make a choice: continue down a passionate path in a dying field, or shift focus to something with less joy in hopes of obtaining a job.

This new generation of college graduates presented a shift in cultural focus as well. Students were less inclined to pursue money, as their parents had done one generation earlier. College graduates entering into the new decade placed a heavy focus on gathering life experience, as opposed to financial wealth. Their parents' generation did not see this cultural shift as valuable. Some students clung to the money-making priorities of their parents, while others made choices that led toward experience, travel, and wisdom.

Benjamin Emerson was forced to confront this cultural shift. He had made difficult decisions throughout his young life; however, no decision would impact him or those he encountered any more than this single, seemingly simple choice.

# CHAPTER 1

Ben shot up in his bed and his heart began to quicken pace. *What was that noise?* He looked around his fraternity bedroom. An Irish flag hung on one wall, opposed by a Bob Marley poster with the lyrics to *One Love* embedded in the backdrop. A Canon Rebel camera sat atop a bookshelf that overflowed with history books and Ernest Hemingway novels. A lacrosse stick rested against the left side of the faded blue couch. Ben's head throbbed slightly, a result of one too many beers during last night's college graduation party.

The wall clock read *8:03 a.m.* When Ben's cell phone rang for a second time, he threw his covers to the side and stepped across his room to the desk. He didn't recognize the phone number, but he figured that anybody who called this early on his college graduation day must need something important.

"Hello?" Ben answered.

"Hi, I'm calling for Benjamin Emerson," said a man's

voice on the other end of the phone.

"This is him," Ben said.

"Great," the man said. "I'm Martin Smith, Recruitment Director for Portland Public Relations. How are you doing this morning?"

"I'm doing well," Ben said.

He grabbed his temples with his free hand. His head still pounded, but he feigned professionalism. A sunbeam snuck through the closed blinds and caught Ben in the eye, making him wince.

"Good," Mr. Smith said. "I'm calling to discuss your current job offer with our public relations firm."

"Yeah, I'm really excited to start my job next week," Ben said. "I've wanted to work for Portland PR since I began working on my journalism degree at University of Oregon. You can't beat a chance to work with some of *your*...I mean *our* clients."

"I'm glad you think highly of our firm and our client list," Mr. Smith said, "but I have some unfortunate news for you."

Ben's heart sunk. His breathing quickened as he forgot about his headache. The tone in Mr. Smith's voice sounded ominous. Ben sat on his bed and took a deep breath in an attempt to compose himself.

"Though we were thrilled to offer you the job of Secondary Copywriter," Mr. Smith continued, "we regret to inform you that the position is no longer needed."

"What are you saying?" Ben asked.

"I'm sorry, Mr. Emerson," Mr. Smith said. "We won't be needing you at this point in time."

"Why?" Ben asked. "I don't understand. What did I do

wrong?"

"You did nothing wrong, Mr. Emerson," Mr. Smith said. "Unfortunately, with the economy the way it is, we've had to make some budget cuts here at Portland PR. And, as it pertain to you, we decided that we can't afford to hire another copywriter right now. We simply don't have the budget for it."

"I understand," Ben said.

"Good luck with your future and we hope you find something that interests you as you prepare to leave college," Mr. Smith said.

"Thanks," Ben said awkwardly.

"We appreciate your understanding," Mr. Smith said. "Goodbye."

Ben tossed his phone onto his bed and buried his face in his hands. His face felt hot and he began to sweat from emotional distress. He thought about crying, but he suppressed his sadness and transformed it into anger. Though his phone call had been disconnected for longer than a minute, he cursed Portland Public Relations and Mr. Smith. He stood and kicked a soccer ball as hard as he could. The ball rebounded off the wall and hit him in the chest, but he didn't care.

He looked in the mirror that hung on his door. His dark brown hair was messy and he had bags under his eyes, a direct result of little sleep. He rubbed his eyes and ran his fingers along his thick, dark eyebrows. Feeling his face, Ben realized that he needed to shave before graduation. He wanted to exercise, but his slight hangover and sudden unemployment impeded his usual morning motivation to complete a series of push-ups, sit-ups, and pull-ups, so he settled for a strenuous toe-touch to stretch his stiff legs. As he rose, he looked in the mirror again, this time fighting back tears.

All he wanted to do was forgo his graduation ceremony and lie next to his girlfriend, Samantha Van Miller. She had an ability to shake him from any moment of weakness. Though brash, she often forced Ben to realize that his emotions were holding him back. Samantha was ambitious and saw only her goals. Sometimes, Ben enjoyed that quality; other times, he wished that she was more free-flowing and tender-hearted. But, she was beautiful and she wanted to be with Ben after college graduation.

The thought of having a woman who genuinely cared for him and wanted to be with him made Ben blinded by love. Or, what he perceived to be love. Ben's friends had tried to tell him that he could do better, but when friends encourage their friends to date other people, they can approach the subject too gingerly and the message does not sink as well as it should.

Ben daydreamed about the harsh comfort of Samantha, but knew he would see her later. He showered and returned to his room. He pulled a blue dress shirt from his closet. *Matches my mood*, he thought. He grabbed a red tie and looked in the mirror to tie it. Without a knock, Ben's door opened and Chris walked in dressed in a suit.

"Good morning!" Chris shouted.

"What's up, man?" Ben said.

"I'm just ready to graduate and move on to bigger and better things," Chris said. "Aren't you?"

"Yeah," Ben said. "I guess."

Ben and Chris walked down the stairs. Ben looked at

their fraternity's golden Greek letters that hung above the front door. He thought about the memories that his college experience brought; most included Chris.

Ben and Chris met four years earlier on their first day of college. Chris' parents flew with him in order to assist his transition to university life. Ben arrived on the train. When he climbed the stairs to their dorm room with his backpack and single box, Chris was hanging a poster above the door frame; the university randomly paired the two boys together as dorm roommates.

They became friends quickly, as they bonded over mutual interests: attending college football games, drinking beer, and having fun in any situation. Since Chris' family lived on the opposite side of the country, they often spent holidays together. During their first term of college, they decided to join the same fraternity, which strengthened their bonds of friendship by allowing them to realize that they shared the same core values of courage, honesty, and intellect.

As they progressed through college, their academic interests veered dramatically, but they remained close friends through extracurricular activities. They attended every fraternity social event together, which built lasting memories. They served as sound boards for one another when unfortunate situations with girls arose, which happened frequently. They accumulated varying interests, but their core values cemented their bond as friends.

When Chris achieved a perfect score on his senior accounting final test, Ben met him across the street from campus to buy him a whiskey shot. When the school newspaper published Ben's first article on the front page,

Chris took him out for a congratulatory beer. The two friends supported one another's goals, even though their particular interests did not align. They were able to try out their talents in the safety of the university setting. And they succeeded. The success of one friend usually lead to the influenced success of the other.

Now, the safety of academia and the worry-free lifestyle that Ben possessed for the past four years was evaporating. The real world beckoned and it terrified him.

The sun began to warm the Oregon spring air, but the chill of morning dew still lingered. Evergreen trees and newly-leaved oaks filled empty spaces between single-story restaurants and students houses. The tree-lined sidewalks provided frequent shady spots that fluctuated the boys' temperatures; Ben felt more awake when the cool breeze blew.

"This could be our last walk to campus," Ben said.

"It'll be my last walk to campus," Chris said, "and I couldn't be happier."

"How can you say that, dude?" Ben asked.

"At this time next month, I'll be walking down Wall Street in New York City," Chris said. "Every morning, I'll grab my Starbuck's coffee and stroll down Broadway in my three-piece suit. I'll turn left on Wall Street and walk into JP Morgan Chase like I own the place. Every month, I'll receive a paycheck that could pay for a full four-year college tuition. I'll be rolling in money!"

Chris smiled and quickened his pace in a subconscious effort to reach the graduation stadium quicker. Ben slowed his stroll and looked at the ground.

"What's wrong, Ben?" Chris said.

"Portland PR called this morning," Ben said.

"Did they offer to pay you even more for your copywriting position?" Chris asked.

"Actually," Ben said, "they eliminated my position. They fired me before I even started."

"Damn, Ben. I'm sorry, buddy," Chris said.

"Me too," Ben said. "I worked so hard to acquire that job. I drove up to Portland five times for interview rounds and tests. I put all my job-seeking effort into that position. Now what am I going to do?"

# CHAPTER 2

The boys walked silently for a while; Chris felt guilty for gloating about his promising future, while Ben felt the wounds of failure and uncertainty. They passed Hayward Field, the famous track-and-field stadium where Steve Prefontaine enshrined his cross-country legacy in the 1970s. Taking a shortcut through the Bean dormitories, Ben and Chris arrived at Matthew Knight Arena. The new basketball arena felt imposing. Its sleek metal frame and massive windows demonstrated architectural ingenuity. It stood as a symbol of the futuristic, forward-thinking direction that the university was headed.

"Here we go," Chris said.

He took his first step on the rising staircase to the stadium.

"Happy graduation day, my man," Ben said.

They walked through the immense double doors and immersed themselves into the crowd of familiar graduates. Ben found some other fraternity members near the trophy case display, so he and Chris fell in line with them. Ben looked for Samantha, but was unable to find her in the crowd of 5,000 students. Somehow, he lost motivation to prioritize her during a graduation ceremony that he lamented. The group made its way to the stadium floor and found chairs near the center aisle.

"My parents are sitting up there in the front row with their cameras," Chris said.

Ben turned to look. Chris' parents waved to the boys, so the boys reciprocated.

"Is your mom here?" Chris asked.

"No," Ben said. "She couldn't afford the flight from New York. She hasn't landed an acting job in a few months, so she's operating on a tight budget these days. I haven't talked to her since she told me that last month."

"That's too bad," Chris said. "You can come to dinner with my family tonight if you want."

"Thanks," Ben said.

The President of the University of Oregon walked onto the graduation stage and congratulated the students for their time and dedication to academia. The commencement speaker was introduced and he walked to the podium to begin his speech. He introduced himself as a former lawyer and a congressional candidate in the upcoming elections in November. The speaker rambled for 30 minutes and ended with a cheesy send-off tagline.

"Now, go forth and change the world," the speaker announced. "The future is yours for the taking."

"Damn right it is," Chris said.

"What future?" Ben muttered.

The speaker received an applause. A university official

took the stage and began to announce names of the graduates. The university's president positioned himself at the end of the stage walkway where he would give students their diplomas and pose for a photograph.

"*James Phillip Anderson*," the announcer said.

James Phillip Anderson walked across the stage with a wide smile and made long strides to the president to receive his diploma. More student names were called. Eventually, Ben and Chris' middle row rose and walked to the stage entrance.

"*Benjamin Francis Emerson*," the announcer said.

Ben felt a sudden shortness of breath. He walked up the steps to the stage and looked out at the crowd. The rows of graduates seemed never-ending as they faded into the stadium spotlights. Parents and extended family members packed the upper decks of the arena to watch their loved ones graduate. Ben thought about his mother and wished she could have made the flight. He thought about his father and wished that he was still alive.

The president stood at the other end of the walkway with a diploma and an outstretched hand. Ben walked toward him. As he strode across the stage, a feeling of pride surged through him, yet he felt a sensation of failure for his projected future. With every step, Ben's sentiments of success shifted toward feelings of failure. By the time he reached the other end of the stage, he felt downtrodden. Ben grabbed his diploma, shook the president's hand, and walked off of the stage. His head began to hang.

"*Christopher Andrew Morgan*," the announcer said.

Chris walked across the stage with East Coast precision to receive his diploma. His immaculately combed blonde hair stuck out of his graduation cap. Chris felt a sense of complete accomplishment for both his performance in college academics and his success in finding a high-paying career. His confidence bordered on arrogance, which reflected in his strut toward his diploma.

He followed Ben to their row of chairs and they both sat and high-fived each other. After the final student walked across the stage, the announcer congratulated the group once more and every student threw their graduation caps into the air. Ben and Chris followed the crowd through the main arena doors and congregated outside while they waited for Chris' parents.

"Christopher!" shouted Chris' mother as she ran to meet him. "I'm so proud of you."

Chris' mom hugged him. His dad followed with another hug of pride.

"Ben," Chris' dad said, "it's good to see you again. Congratulations."

"Thank you, Mr. Morgan," Ben said.

"Well," Mrs. Morgan said, "Where should we go for dinner?"

"I asked our hotel concierge and he told me that the most expensive steakhouse in town is nearby," Mr. Morgan said.

"Only the best for our boy," Mrs. Morgan said.

Ben felt awkward, unsure if Chris' invitation to dinner still applied.

"Ben," Mrs. Morgan continued, "where are your parents?"

"They weren't able to be here today," Ben said.

Mrs. Morgan looked at her husband with pity and then

back at Ben.

"Would you like to come to dinner with us?" she asked.

"Thanks," Ben said. "I would love to."

Ben walked behind Chris and his family as they strolled down the street to the restaurant. He felt happy to have a family to be with on his graduation day, but he felt like an imposition on Chris' family. They entered the steakhouse and sat at a round table. Ben looked at his place setting and noticed that he had three forks, two spoons, and a red cloth napkin. *What do I do with this many forks*, Ben thought.

The waiter brought four menus to the table and described the daily specials with eloquence. The number of French words in the waiter's description suggested an aura of superiority in the restaurant. Ben looked at the menu and his eyes focused on the price of each item first. He was shocked. There was no way he could afford even a side salad, not to mention a full meal at this place. He began to panic.

"Ben," Mr. Morgan said, "we're paying for your dinner, just so you're aware. This is a big day for you and you need to celebrate, so order anything you want."

"Are you sure?" Ben asked.

"Of course," Mr. Morgan said.

"Thank you, sir," Ben said. "You have no idea how much I appreciate that."

Ben hated accepting financial pity from people who had money. He knew that part of Mr. Morgan's offer came from generosity, but the offer was underlined with pity and fueled with superiority. Ben's financial stature had crippled his confidence since he became old enough to compare himself with his peers; however, acquiring mass amounts of wealth never drew his interest because he saw how money changed people's behavior.

Ben ordered his favorite beer, a porter crafted at a brewery down the street. Chris ordered a steak, so Ben did the same. Steak was Ben's favorite food. Chris and his family discussed the happenings of the Morgan's Boston neighborhood, effectively excluding Ben from participating in the conversation. Ben had never been anywhere outside of the state of Oregon.

Though Ben had met Chris' parents once before, he knew they were sophisticated and worldly, or at least gave off that appearance. Mr. Morgan's sleek suit and Mrs. Morgan's massive diamond ring suggested that they had old money. Mr. Morgan was a financial advisor in Boston and Mrs. Morgan was a professor at Boston College. They were kind, but they portrayed a carefully crafted image of high society.

"Chris," Mr. Morgan said, "when does your job on Wall Street begin?"

"I start in three weeks," Chris said. "I'm packing my car tonight and I'm driving to New York in the morning. With stops, the 3,000-mile journey should take about one week."

"Do you have a place to live in Manhattan yet?" Mrs. Morgan asked.

"I do," Chris said. "The company is paying for a loft in the city for me. It's already set."

"That's great, son," Mr. Morgan said. "Have you talked to them about your salary yet?"

"Of course, dad," Chris said. "I have a huge salary, plus commission."

"Good, son," Mr. Morgan said. "And your retirement

package?"

"I have a 401K and stock purchasing options," Chris said.

"Christopher, my boy, you're set for life," Mr. Morgan said.

The waiter brought the meals to the table. He served Mrs. Morgan first, followed by Mr. Morgan. Ben was served last. Mrs. Morgan cut a small piece from her steak and took a dainty bite. She sipped her red wine with dignity. Ben took a big gulp of beer and watched the Morgan family as they progressed through the multitude of silverware options and precise napkin usage.

"Now, Ben," Mrs. Morgan said, "where were your parents today?"

Chris looked awkwardly at Ben, for he knew the full story. Chris turned red with embarrassment and couldn't believe he forgot to mention Ben's family situation to his mother.

"Well," Ben said.

He was used to this question at this point in his life.

"My mom lives in New York City. I haven't talked to her in a while, but she hasn't landed any acting gigs in a few months and couldn't afford the flight out to the West Coast."

"You mother is an actor?" Mr. Morgan asked. "Would we recognize her from any films?"

"No," Ben said. "She acts in small theatre plays in New York. When I went to college, she left Portland to pursue her dream of becoming a Broadway actor. She hasn't made it to Broadway yet, but she keeps trying. We don't talk much, but I admire her passion, I guess."

"Did your father move to New York with her?" Mrs. Morgan asked.

"No," Ben said.

He looked down at his food. Though he was used to this question, it still made him depressed.

"My dad died in Iraq when I was in high school."

"I'm so sorry, Ben," Mr. Morgan said.

"Me too," Ben said. "He was one of the first troops deployed to Iraq when President George Bush sent the military to the Middle East after the attacks on the World Trade Center. He returned from that deployment, but he was sent back to Iraq in 2006 and was killed by accidental friendly fire."

"Ben," Mrs. Morgan said, "I'm so sorry."

"It's life," Ben said.

The whole table was silent for some time. The Morgan parents didn't quite know what to say to ease their own sense of awkwardness. Chris looked at Ben, who was staring at his plate. Ben wondered what to say to relieve the tension at the table. He cut a small piece from his steak and chewed it. The medium-rare steak juice flowed over his tongue. Ben stabbed at his spinach salad and took a bite of leaves. The vinegar-based dressing electrified his dry lips. Mr. Morgan broke the silence.

"Well, Ben, "Mr. Morgan said. "What's next for you? Did you find a job?"

"I did," Ben said. "Portland Public Relations offered me a job as a copywriter."

"That's great!" Mrs. Morgan said, overenthusiastically to cover her lingering sense of awkwardness.

"Does that match your college major?" Mr. Morgan

asked.

"It did," Ben said. "I studied journalism and history."

"Wonderful," Mr. Morgan said. "When do you start your new life as a college graduate?"

"Good question," Ben said. "Portland PR called this morning and revoked my job position, so I don't know what I'm going to do now. Or where I'm going to go."

Mr. Morgan coughed as he took a bite of steak. Mrs. Morgan looked at her husband with an expression of sympathy for Ben. Chris placed his fork on his plate, took a sip of water, and looked at his parents in embarrassment.

"Do you have a girlfriend, Ben," Mrs. Morgan said, in an attempt to lighten the mood.

"I do," Ben said. "Her name's Samantha. She's from Portland. Real pretty girl."

He took another bite of steak and chewed it quickly so that he could continue talking.

"And what is her plan after graduation?" Mr. Morgan asked.

"Well, she has a few options," Ben said. "Her first choice is to work for a non-profit organization in Portland, which would be great because we're staying together after college. She'll be the only thing tying me to the Pacific Northwest at this point. Plus, I love her family and I want to be a part of it someday, since I don't really have one of my own."

Chris rolled his eyes. He disapproved of Ben's ties to Samantha.

"She has another job offer in Miami," Ben said. "A major news station offered her a job as a television reporter. But, she's not into fame and glory, so I'm confident she'll take the job in Portland."

Chris looked emphatically at his parents.

"I told Ben that he should move to New York with me and search for writing and public relations jobs there," Chris said. "But, *Samantha* wouldn't let him."

"She would let me," Ben said. "I just don't want to go to New York because I'm committed to her."

"Well, get un-committed and drive out to the City with me tomorrow morning," Chris said.

"I can't, man," Ben said. "At this point, I've got to follow Samantha."

Chris rolled his eyes again.

A feeling of confinement swept over Ben. He began to feel hopeless. He had no job, no future, no plan, aside from following his girlfriend to his own hometown, which was beginning to feel like her hometown.

Ben stood and excused himself. He felt hot and embarrassed, so he walked to the hostess and asked her to locate the restroom. She pointed to the back of the restaurant, so Ben strolled that direction. He pushed the door open and looked around the men's restroom to ensure that he was alone. A wall-to-wall mirror hung above the sink. Ben walked to it and made eye contact with himself, but feelings of inadequacy crept to the surface and he broke his gaze. He turned on the sink and splashed some cold water on his face, but dried it with a paper towel quickly to avoid dampening his shirt from water drops.

After calming himself, Ben returned to the dinner table. He made eye contact with Mrs. Morgan, who stopped speaking immediately. Ben looked at Chris and his expression indicated that the Morgan family had been discussing Ben's history the entire time he was away from the table.

The server brought the check and Mr. Morgan grabbed it with a sense of urgency. He left a large sum of cash as a tip while standing, which indicated that dinner was over. Ben followed the Morgan family through the front door of the restaurant and stopped near the parking lot.

"Thank you for dinner," Ben said

"You're welcome, honey," Mrs. Morgan said.

"It was nice to see you," Ben said. "Have a safe trip back to Boston."

Ben shook Mr. Morgan's hand and hugged Chris' mother. Ben took a few steps back in order to give Chris some space to speak with his parents before they returned to Boston. The Morgans said goodbye to Chris and waved to Ben. Chris turned to meet him and the boys began their walk back to campus.

"So, Ben," Chris said. "What *is* your plan?"

"What do you mean?" Ben said.

"You know, now that you don't have to move back to Portland and work for Portland PR," Chris said.

"I don't have a plan, man," Ben said. "I'm just excited that Samantha is probably deciding to stay in Portland so that she can stay with me and chase her dreams of helping people."

Chris continued to walk, but he paused his demeanor and thought. Ben could sense Chris' thought process. After living together for four years of college, the friends had developed an innate ability to read each other's facial expressions.

"How much money do you have to your name?" Chris asked.

"Enough to survive for a few weeks, I guess," Ben said.

Ben worked as an academic tutor for student athletes four days per week through college in order to pay for rent, food, and the occasional night at the bar with his friends. His tuition was paid through scholarships and government grants, so Ben accrued no student loan debt during his time at the university. Since his parents were not able to contribute any money toward his college tuition, he found a way for the government to pay for most of it.

Chris' parents paid for their son's tuition. He didn't work during college, aside from one summer job spent working as an intern for a financial company's accounting department. When Ben and Chris went to bars on the weekends, Chris bought the first round of drinks, and usually the second.

"Do you have any reason to stay in Oregon?" Chris asked.

"Well," Ben said. He paused and thought for a minute. "Just Samantha. I mean, my family doesn't live there anymore. Aside from nostalgia, I have no more ties to the city."

"Then come to New York with me," Chris said.

"I don't have enough money to live in New York," Ben said. "Nor do I have enough money to travel to across the country to the City."

Ben paused. He knew he was forgetting another reason.

"Plus, Samantha wouldn't approve," Ben said.

"First of all, don't worry about the money," Chris said. "My Wall Street firm is paying for my trip out there. I'm driving in my Jeep, so they're paying for gas money and food."

Ben nodded.

"Second," Chris said, "dump Samantha. She's not even nice to you."

"But we've been together for two years, dude," Ben said. "Plus, she's demonstrating generosity by staying in Portland so that we can stay together."

"Whatever, man," Chris said. "Just know that the offer is on the table. Samantha is the only thing holding you back from moving out there with me."

Ben stewed as he walked. He remained silent for over two minutes. He wanted to find other reasons to decline Chris' New York offer so that he did not appear like he was controlled by a dictator of a girlfriend.

"So I wouldn't have to pay to travel to New York at all?" Ben asked.

"Nope," Chris said. "My company would have to pay that fee anyways."

"What about when I arrive in New York?" Ben asked. "How will I afford to live there? The cost of living in that city is enormous."

Chris paused and thought. Suddenly, his pondering frown turned into an enlightened smile.

"My company is paying for my downtown apartment," Chris said. "You can live with me until you find a job and a place to live."

"I don't want to impose on your new life, man," Ben said.

"You wouldn't be imposing," Chris said. "Besides, you're brilliant. You'll find a job in no time."

Ben and Chris walked through campus. They passed the quad; the Knight Library lit up as the sun faded. On the opposing end of the grass walkway, the Lillis Business

Complex illuminated from the inside; its glass exterior exposed its inner workings. The rising lights of the museum produced a gothic cathedral atmosphere. Spring trees stilled in the evening air. The sun set behind the west side of campus as the boys continued their journey east.

"Well, I'm jumping in my Jeep and driving to New York around sunrise tomorrow," Chris said. "I have an open seat. What do you think?"

"It sounds like a fun adventure," Ben said, "but I just can't go. Samantha means the world to me and she provides me with a family and emotional security. I can't just ditch her and move across the country. I know she wouldn't do that to me if the situation was reversed."

"I understand," Chris said. "When you decide to join me on my cross-country journey, make sure you pack light."

He smiled, half-joking.

The boys walked into the fraternity house walkway, which was dark aside from the mandatory floodlights in the entryway. Samantha was waiting there on a steel bench. Her expression looked grim.

"I'll see you before you leave in the morning," Ben said to Chris.

"Alright, man," Chris said. "Goodnight, Samantha."

She half-smiled at Chris and turned to Ben with a sense of urgency. The house's shadowy interior made her light brown hair seem black. A single overhead light produced shadows on her cheekbones. She creased her lips and formulated her words before she decided to speak.

"Ben, you'd better sit down," Samantha said.

"Why?" Ben asked.

"We need to talk," she said.

"About what?" Ben said.

He felt the pit of his stomach sink; a similar feeling occurred this morning when he lost his job.

"Benny," Samantha said, "I've decided to move to Miami for that reporting job."

Ben stood silently. The news came like a punch to the gut. The news blindsided him.

"I know I've told you that I wanted to help people in Portland and that I don't care about making money, but…"

"But what?" Ben said.

"I was lying to myself. I do want to be rich and famous and Miami is the place to be if I want to achieve those goals."

Ben smiled, but his smile came from pain and personal insecurity. Inside, he felt broken. How could a woman he knew so well make a decision that went against her character?

Or did the decision go against *his* character?

Ben stared through Samantha and into the darkness behind her. He wanted to look into her eyes, but tension and stubborn disappointment impeded his ability to control his gaze, so he settle for looking beyond her.

He remained speechless for what seemed like an hour. Thoughts flowed through in mind, but seemed to leave immediately. His brain whirled and his emotions and rational thoughts clashed, so he turned off his mind and allowed pain to envelop him.

"What will happen with us?" Ben asked, finally breaking the silence.

He knew the response before he asked the question, but he clung to hope that his prediction was wrong.

"Ben," Samantha said, "I'm breaking up with you."

Samantha looked directly at Ben when she made her declaration. She meant it and Ben felt her sincerity.

She saw Ben begin to cry and she turned and left the house. Her figure disappeared into the shadows.

# CHAPTER 3

Tears fell from Ben's eyes. He staggered up the stairs to his bedroom. He felt as if he floated instead of walked. His mind seemed detached from his body. Everything had gone wrong.

He did not want to see another person. Since Ben and Chris were the only two people still living in the usual 40-person house, he figured that would be an easy request to fulfill.

Ben walked into his room and flipped on the light switch. He crashed onto his bed and allowed all of his stress to flow through his body and exhale as tears. He cried. And he cried some more.

He lifted his head and looked at the watermark on his comforter. He sat up and noticed his Bob Marley poster.

A rush of sentimentality came to him, so he opened his window and stepped onto the deck. He found the makeshift wooden ladder and climbed to the flat roof of the house. He crawled to the corner of the roof and sat on the edge. His feet dangled three stories above the sidewalk.

The late-spring air warmed Ben. He looked up and saw stars. The night was clear, unusual for a spring night in the Pacific Northwest. Ben found the Big Dipper and a sudden feeling of smallness overcame him. He looked down toward the street and it no longer seemed like a far fall. He noticed the massive evergreen trees that lined the curbs and embedded themselves in alleyways and in front yards. His eyes continued forward toward the University itself.

Campus sprawled in front of him. He saw the stadium lights from the turf fields and thought about his time as a freshman on the lacrosse team, until he injured his knee and stopped playing. Ben's eyes travelled further. He saw the journalism school's lights, which sparked memories of writing for the school newspaper, *The Oregon Daily Emerald.* He loved writing for the newspaper, but in the era of blogs and electronic publications, the possibility of a future as a newspaper columnist dwindled. Ben squinted to see the history building at the far end of campus, which brought memories of researching the American Civil Rights Movement for his final written thesis.

Ben wished he could see Autzen Stadium, but it was too far in the distance. Autzen Stadium evoked memories of tailgating before football games and spending time with his best friends. He recalled his first experience at an Oregon Duck football tailgate party at which he drank his first beer. The cheap light brew tasted crisp with a hint of maturity and independence. In hindsight, it was the lowest quality beer on the market, but the moment was precious. Chris was by his side, even back then.

In a momentary return to his present state of roof-sitting, Ben realized that he was uncomfortable, so he laid on his back and saw the lights of an airplane move overhead. This sparked thoughts of travel, specifically about his adventures through Europe during his junior year, where he spent six months studying Spanish and history in Spain. The small village of Oviedo taught him to adventure boldly and to seek opportunities that stretched the limits of his comfort zone. He thought of his most vivid memories during his stay in Spain: playing spontaneous soccer matches with the Africans that lived there, reading the newspaper in the corner coffee shop by his antiquated apartment, and the ritualistic Christmas mass at the Catholic cathedral.

Ben assumed that his time in Spain would be the pinnacle of his college existence. After all, he worked overtime all summer at the tutoring center and for the school paper to pay for his overseas tuition and worked as a tutor in Spain to afford weekend *cervezas*, but when he returned to the States, his social résumé continued to grow. When Ben became the President of his fraternity during his senior year, he assumed that public relations firms would call him daily and beg him to write for them. Or *The Oregonian*, perhaps. Maybe even *The New York Times*.

As his thoughts travelled from scintillating college memories to his unpromising future, he jolted upright and became fully aware of the present. The air had chilled. *What was the purpose of all of this?* Ben thought. He wrestled with the reasons he went to college originally. Now that he had completed his educational time allotment, what would he do with it? *How could I have invested so much time, money, and effort into my college education and have no plan for my future?* Ben thought.

After reviewing his most treasured college memories, Ben came to a realization: none of his most treasured memories featured Samantha.

After an hour of deep thinking and reflection, Ben stood and took one last, long look at the University of Oregon. The campus was silent, but bright. He listened intently; he heard no sound of cars, no shouts from students, no music from house parties. Just silence. Beautiful, reflective, quiet. He turned and crawled toward the ladder and descended from the roof.

Ben stepped through the window and into his room and face-planted onto his bed. Thoughts of an uncertain future swirled through his mind. He rolled over and looked at his poster of Bob Marley again and read the song lyrics of *One Love*, which echoed the condition of all humankind and the purpose of human interaction.

He sat on the edge of his bed and looked at the Irish flag. His thoughts turned to his forefathers from Ireland and the unpredictable path that sprouted from an immigration to a new home. He flopped onto his back. The bed bounced as Ben's head nestled into the pillow.

With the lights still on, Ben fell asleep, still questioning his future, let alone tomorrow's decision to move across the country.

# CHAPTER 4

For the second day in a row, Ben awoke to the sound of his phone ringing. He sat up in his bed and realized that he was fully clothed. He swished his tongue around in his mouth and regretted not brushing his teeth before he fell asleep. The shades were open. The sun hadn't risen yet, though its rays crept upon the low, rolling hills.

Ben stood and walked to his phone, which rested in its usual place on the corner of his desk. His eyes adjusted as he looked at his phone screen. *Chris is calling this early?* Ben thought. He picked up his phone and held it to his ear.

"Hey, man," Ben said. His voice was raspy.

"Good morning sunshine," Chris said.

"What's up?" Ben asked.

"I know your answer already, but I need to ask again," Chris said. "Are you coming to New York with me?"

Ben was silent. He wanted Chris to hang up the phone so that he could think about his choice; however, Chris waited and reciprocated the silence from the other end.

Positive and negative outcomes raced through Ben's thoughts as he began to weigh his options. He thought about his ties to Oregon and realized that he had none left. His father was dead. His mother lived in New York City. All of his friends were moving on to careers in various states. Then, he remembered that his relationship with Samantha ended last night.

He thought about his financial availability to move to New York City and decided that he did not have enough money to move anywhere unless someone else assisted him. He had no job, but the prospect of finding a career in Portland looked grim, considering the impact of the economic recession.

His thoughts trailed back toward the fact that his mother lived in New York City. Even though his relationship with her had strained since the death of his father, he could not release the pull toward the East Coast.

"You know what," Ben said, "I'm coming with you. I have no reason to stay in Oregon."

"Wow!" Chris shouted. "Samantha's letting you go?"

"We broke up last night," Ben said. "She's moving to Miami."

"I'm sorry, buddy," Chris said. "I know you're hurting, but I do love this news. She wasn't good to you, man. Come to the City with me and we'll find you a real girl."

"Thanks, Chris."

"Start packing. We leave in an hour."

Ben plugged his phone into the charger and placed it on the desk. He stood and looked around his room. Ben considered himself spontaneous, but a decision of this magnitude required significant forethought. Panic crept into his mind; the lack of preparedness for this journey caused him to regret his decision slightly.

He reached into his closet and grabbed his 55-liter backpack. Its internal frame design served him well when he used it to hike through the Oregon wilderness during weekend adventures. He opened it and shook out some stray leaves and dirt from his last backpacking trip in the forest outside of Eugene. Though he possessed few belongings, the task of packing everything he owned into this backpack seemed daunting.

Starting with the essentials, Ben reached into the top drawer of his dresser and retrieved clean socks and underwear. He placed them neatly on the bed and moved to the second drawer, where he retrieved two pairs of jeans and a pair of black slacks. Shirts, ties, belts, and two pairs of shoes came next. After all of his clothes laid on his bed, Ben rolled them up and compacted each article into his backpack, which still allowed for about ten liters of free space.

Ben moved to his bookshelf. He grabbed his four favorite books: *A People's History of the United States* by Howard Zinn, *The Sun Also Rises* by Ernest Hemingway, *Self-Reliance and Other Essays* by Ralph Waldo Emerson, and *The Bible*. Ben grabbed his Bible and placed on top of the other three books in the top compartment of the pack. Ben saw his Canon Rebel camera on top of the bookshelf, so he placed the camera in its small foam carrying case and hooked it to the outer shell of the backpack. He put two blue-ink pens and his lucky silver dollar into a small hip-strap pocket.

Reaching into a drawer, he found his gold Saint

Christopher medallion and placed the necklace over his head. Ben's father gave the necklace to him at the airport when he left for his first deployment in Iraq. He told Ben that Saint Christopher was the patron saint of travelers; to Ben, this meant that his father would return home safely. Ben wore the medallion every day for four years until his father was killed near Baghdad. Since that day, Ben banished the medallion to his dresser drawer, unable to wear it without a deep feeling of sorrow. Ben felt that sorrow return as he placed the golden Saint Christopher necklace around his neck, but with that pain rushed memories of courage and hope.

Ben looked in the mirror and investigated the visual appeal of the necklace. His eyes travelled upwards toward his head. Since Ben hadn't showered, his hair was messy, so he wore his black-and-red Portland Trail Blazers hat. He flipped the hat around and wore it backwards because he despised the field-of-vision subtraction that a ball cap bill produced. The hat's interior showed signs of wear, but he kept the exterior presentable.

He looked around his room to ensure that he had not forgotten anything. The furniture in his room belonged to his fraternity house. Since Ben's history classes required absurd amounts of reading, Ben had read all of the books on his shelf, so he decided to donate them to the next resident of his room. He filled his 40-ounce steel water bottle from the bathroom sink and shoved it into the side holder of his pack.

Ben threw his backpack over his shoulders. He was surprised that all of his worldly possessions felt lightweight. Grabbing his lacrosse stick with his left hand

and soccer ball with his right, he walked out of his bedroom and closed the door behind him for the last time. He strolled down the hallway to the other end of the house. Chris' door was open, so Ben entered. Two large suitcases and two thick trunks filled Chris' bedroom floor.

"That's all you're bringing?" Chris asked, pointing to Ben's backpack.

"This is all I own," Ben said.

"I guess you took it to heart when I told you to pack light," Chris said with a slight laugh.

"Is that all you're bringing?" Ben said sarcastically.

"I hope all my junk fits in the Jeep," Chris said.

Chris looked at his packing materials and measured with his eyes.

"Are you ready to roll?" Ben asked.

"Yes, sir," Chris said. "Let's pack the Jeep."

Chris brought one trunk downstairs and placed it in the back of the car. Ben followed with another trunk. Chris' suitcases went in the back seat, along with Ben's backpack. Chris slammed the Jeep's trunk flap and tested it to ensure the safety of his possessions.

The headlights of the Jeep glared at the road. Its grill snarled with the added weight of trunks and suitcases. The beige ragtop accented the forest green paint and the tires personified rugged adventure. The spare tire on the back of the Jeep gave Ben and Chris an added sense of security.

"Maybe we can drive with the ragtop down once we reach Montana," Chris suggested. "I checked the weather and we're supposed to run into some light rain until we leave Washington."

Ben looked toward the park across the street and saw the

sun begin to rise over the massive evergreen trees. He heard spring birds chirp from the park. He wondered how light rain could occur on such a fresh spring morning, but he knew that Pacific Northwest weather changed minute-by-minute.

Ben turned and took a farewell glance at the fraternity house. Though Ben did not notice, Chris did the same. The boys jumped into their seats; Chris sat in the driver seat and Ben in the passenger seat. Chris handed a paper map of the United States to Ben, which he placed in the door's side panel.

Chris inserted an album into the car stereo's interface and turned up the volume. A 1990s hip-hop beat thumped through the speakers. The beat reminded Ben and Chris of a specific college house party from earlier that year, so they looked at each other and laughed as they waited for the lyrics to begin.

"Well, Ben," Chris said. "Shall we?"

"Let's get this show on the road," Ben said. He laughed lightly at his own usage of the cliché.

The Jeep pulled out of the fraternity parking lot and drove two blocks before stopping at a coffee shop. Both Ben and Chris drank coffee every morning, so they ordered two black coffees with a dash of milk and placed their drinks in the Jeep's cup holders. Chris shifted from neutral to first gear and exited the coffee shop drive-through lane and entered the main campus thoroughfare. The Jeep passed a large green sign that read "The University of Oregon" and turned left onto Franklin Street.

"It's been a wild ride at this school, hasn't it?" Ben said.

"Yes it has," Chris said. "I'm glad that we made it

through all four years with so much life experience."

"Me too," Ben said. "That life experience worked out much better for you, though."

"Why?" Chris asked. "Just because it landed me a job?"

"Exactly," Ben said. "My college experience didn't get me a damn thing."

"I just knew exactly what I wanted at the end of my college education," Chris said. "All you need is a plan."

"You're probably right," Ben said. "What was your plan, exactly?"

"I knew that I wanted to make as much money as possible when I graduated," Chris continued. "I followed the money and it led me to Wall Street, so that's where I needed to be."

"I don't need piles of money to make me happy, though," Ben said.

"Sure you do," Chris said.

An hour passed and the mixtape in the stereo was nearing its end. The Jeep merged onto Interstate 5 and continued for over an hour until it veered east on Interstate 84. Since it was still early, the boys evaded heavy Portland traffic.

Ben gazed at the view that the windshield provided. The highway lined the Columbia River, which reflected the sunrise. As the boys passed Multnomah Falls in the Columbia River Gorge, Ben reached into the back seat and grabbed his camera case. He retrieved his camera and held it to his eye. He adjusted the camera's settings to a high shutter speed in order to capture a sharp photograph, even when the Jeep moved at 65 miles per hour. He snapped a few photographs of the 620-foot waterfall with its evergreen backdrop and iconic bridge and sifted through them on his camera's screen to select the photograph with the highest quality and most accurate framing.

"That's a good idea," Chris said. "You should take pictures of every cool feature we pass while we drive."

"I might as well," Ben said. "I didn't take photojournalism classes for nothing."

The Jeep continued through the Columbia Gorge and Ben photographed the scenery. He took a picture of a speed limit sign with a steep cliff in the background. He captured another frame with the highway lining the sparkling river. He snapped a photograph of Chris in-focus with the river blurred in the backdrop. He showed the picture to Chris, who quickly took his eye off the road and looked at the picture.

"That's a good picture," Chris said. "How'd you get so good at photography?"

"Aside from two photojournalism classes," Ben said, "I was a photographer for the *Oregon Daily Emerald*, but I thought I was a better writer than photographer, so I started focusing more on writing articles as college moved forward. For two football games during our sophomore year, I got media passes and took pictures of the games for the *Emerald* from the sideline. I practiced faced-paced photography, so I think that will translate well with our fast-motion Jeep down the freeway."

The Jeep rounded a curve in the highway that followed a protruding cliff. As the rock wall faded behind the Jeep, the eastern sky came into focus. The glistening sunrise began to darken. A black wall of solid clouds moved toward them. Soon, Ben and Chris saw only black sky in their path.

"Those clouds look nasty," Chris said.

"Yeah, but a little Oregon rain never hurt anybody," Ben said.

Chris opened a bag of barbecue-flavored sunflower seeds and shoved a pile into his mouth. His coffee cup was empty, so he used the cup as a spitter for his empty seeds. He offered some to Ben, who took a handful.

As Chris spit his first sunflower seed into his empty cup, a raindrop hit the windshield. Another drop followed, and another, and another. Chris turned on the windshield wipers to a low speed, but before Chris spit another sunflower seed into his cup, he needed the highest speed his Jeep's wipers could produce. Light rain turned into a downpour.

"It's like God turned on the shower," Ben said.

"For real," Chris said. "I can barely see out of the windshield."

Chris' knuckles turned white gradually as his grip on the steering wheel tightened. The Jeep passed a semi-truck and the spray from the truck's wheels flooded the windshield further. Ben grew nervous in the passenger seat.

"Damn, man," Chris said. "I can't see. The rain is too thick."

Ben and Chris flinched as they heard a thunder clap, followed abruptly by a lightning flash. The Jeep's windshield wipers sloshed through the floods on the windshield.

"I'm getting pretty nervous," Chris said. "This ragtop is blowing in the wind and hope it doesn't start to leak. I don't want to lose control and take us off the road."

"If you need to pull off on the next exit, I wouldn't mind," Ben said.

"I don't think I could see a road sign through this rain,"

Chris said.

Instinctively, Ben reached for his Saint Christopher medal. He placed his hand on it and a sudden calm overcame him.

"We'll be alright, Chris," Ben said. "We'll pass Mount Hood soon and the clouds should stop."

As soon as Ben finished speaking, the downpour turned to drizzle, and then to a light sprinkle. Ben looked to the Columbia River and saw a rainbow forming. The clouds passed the Jeep and sunbeams hit the highway, causing steam to rise.

"That was intense," Chris said. "I'm sorry that I panicked."

"It's fine," Ben said. "I was nervous too."

"Thanks for keeping me calm," Chris said.

A familiar hip-hop song resounded through the Jeep's cockpit; the album had completed a full cycle, so Chris ejected it and placed it in the glovebox. As he fished for a new CD, Ben laughed.

"Have we exhausted all of our music options already?" Ben asked.

Chris slammed the glovebox shut. His jaw clenched.

"We only brought four CDs and we've listened to all of them!" Chris shouted. "How could I have overlooked road trip music? I had every detail planned, except for the damn music."

"Well," Ben said, "I guess we'll know the words to every song on these four CDs by the end of our adventure."

Chris smirked, displeased with Ben's eternal optimism, yet grateful for another perspective on the situation. Ben possessed the ability to find a positive twist in every circumstance, while Chris regularly exhibited a sense of pessimistic realism in his demeanor.

As the Jeep passed the Cascade Mountains, the sky cleared. Chris looked in his rear view mirror and saw the dark cloud move further west, away from his precious Jeep. The sky ahead looked clear and warm.

"Benny, how are you holding up with the whole Samantha thing?" Chris asked.

"I'm pretty devastated, to tell you the truth," Ben said. "I thought she was the one."

"No way," Chris said. "I never thought she was the one for you."

"Why not?"

"She never supported your dreams and ambitions," Chris said.

"How so?"

"Remember that time when we were at Taylor's drinking some beer and you said that you were going to interview with a small-town newspaper for a reporting position because it had always been your dream to be a writer? What did she say?"

Ben smiled at the hindsight of his memory.

"She told me that I was an idiot for wanting to be a writer and that I would never make anything of myself if I pursued a job in writing," Ben said.

"And that wasn't the only time she tried to mold you and crush your dreams, right?"

"You're right, man," Ben said. "I guess I was so blinded by her perceived commitment that I couldn't see the truth."

Ben halfway believed his own words. Still, he felt a deep pain at the thought of the loss of Samantha. *Maybe I'll still end up with her*, he thought.

Ben stared out the front windshield. In the distance, mounds appeared; tall, unnatural earthen mounds in symmetrical rows lined the horizon as far as the boys could see. As the Jeep moved closer to the mounds, the size of the physical features seemed to grow. Chris noticed a single-level shack next to a dirt mound and he realized that each pile of earth was taller than the hut.

"What the hell?" Chris said. "What are those things?"

"These dirt piles?" Ben asked.

"Yeah," Chris said. "There's nothing around for miles except giant mounds of dirt. Where are we? The moon?"

"Umatilla," Ben said.

Chris looked at Ben with a perplexed expression.

"Alright, Oregon boy," Chris said. "What's Uma-tilla?"

Ben reached into a memory of a road trip that he and his father had taken to the Umatilla military base when Ben was a child.

With Chris listening actively, Ben explained that the Umatilla military base stored chemical weapons during World War Two. After the war, the nerve gas sat untouched underneath the mounds until the early 2000s when an environmentalist initiative enacted a procedure to destroy the chemicals.

"Why'd they call it Uma-tilla?" Chris asked. "Was that an army general?"

"The Umatilla people were Native Americans who lived on this land," Ben said.

"Why did an Indian tribe want U.S. chemical weapons on their land?" Chris asked.

"Well, they didn't want chemical weapons on their land,

I'm sure," Ben said. "That's the curse of Native American history. The U.S. government didn't care. They rounded up all the Umatilla people, killed the ones who resisted, and forced the rest onto a reservation, which was useless land to the U.S. government anyway. Our government took this land for its own use."

"So the U.S. government replaced a Native American tribe with chemical weapon mounds?" Chris said.

"Basically," Ben said. "Isn't it ironic that a group of peaceful, environmentally friendly people were ousted and replaced with harmful chemicals used for war?"

"Well, I'm glad we got some use out of the land," Chris said.

Ben felt unsure whether Chris intended sarcasm or honest opinion. Ben knew that Chris had a dry sense of humor, so he decided to chuckle with hope that Chris intended sarcasm.

As the Jeep neared the end of the Umatilla mounds, Ben snapped a few photographs of the barren, Martian landscape. He checked his camera's viewing screen and looked at his pictures with semi-approval. The mounds faded into the horizon behind the Jeep.

The boys sped through Washington, passing Gonzaga University in Spokane. Ben photographed a sign that read *Welcome to Idaho* and turned off his camera. He reached into his door's side panel and checked the folded paper map. The boys just entered northern Idaho and were on a trajectory through the state's panhandle.

After leaving the destitute, brown dust bowl of Umatilla, northern Idaho was Eden. Interstate 90 led the Jeep along the shores of Lake Coeur d'Alene for miles. The deep blue water reflected the pending sunset; the lush green forest invited dreams of rustic vacations.

Ben imagined Ralph Waldo Emerson or Henry David Thoreau living in the surrounding wilderness and composing thoughts and philosophies of self-reliance. *A Western Walden Pond*, Ben thought. He desired to live in the way that these enlightened thinkers did long ago, but knew that modern-day pace would not allow that to occur.

Ben snapped a photograph of the *Welcome to Montana* road sign. The action made Chris escape from his driving daydream. The boys realized that they drove through Idaho for an hour in silence, absorbing the forest.

"Sorry, man," Chris said. "I was in deep thought."

"So was I," Ben said. "The wilderness has that effect."

Chris increased the volume of *CD Number One*. The sun began to set, but two hours of daylight remained, which was Chris' estimated time of arrival in Butte, Montana. The Jeep anticipated the day's stopping point.

"We need to find a gas station soon," Chris said. "In the next ten minutes, I hope."

"I haven't seen one since we entered Montana," Ben said.

"I haven't seen any signs of civilization since we left Coeur d'Alene, and that was 60 miles ago," Chris said.

The gas tank gauge dropped below the empty indicator. The gas light flashed for 20 miles. Not wanting to panic again, Chris downplayed his fear of running out of gas in the middle of the Montana wilderness, though this fear became more likely with every tire rotation.

Five minutes passed. Chris looked left into a clearing and saw a massive red sign that hung from two 40-foot logs:

*Montana Mudfest.*

"We're in luck!" Chris shouted. "The Mudfest is this weekend."

"What the hell is the Montana Mudfest?" Ben asked.

"Who knows?" Chris said. "But I'll bet there's a gas station nearby."

The Jeep exited the highway and followed a forested back road, which led to the Montana Mudfest sign. From the windshield, the boys saw massive dirt ramps and mud-filled raceways. Eight mud-splattered monster trucks hibernated just outside of the racetrack.

The Jeep pulled into a gas station, which happened to be the only building in the town. Ben looked at a sign and noticed that the town had a population of 27 people. The gas station served as a restaurant, a grocery store, and a dentist. Based on the gas station attendant's teeth, Chris decided that the dentist's office no longer operated.

Ben filled the gas tank. He needed to practice this skill, since Oregon state law prohibited civilians from pumping their own gas. The toothless, overall-clad attendant noticed the two city boys and he strolled their direction. Another bearded man exited a monster truck with a shotgun in his hand.

"We've got us some city folk!" the bearded man shouted to the attendant.

"Let's get out of here," Chris said to Ben.

Honest panic accompanied his suggestion. Ben took the driver's seat and the boys sped along the back road. The Jeep hugged the road as Ben bolted around its corners and onto Interstate 90.

The sunset was complete by the time the Jeep reached

Butte. Orange streetlights flickered on as Ben and Chris drove through downtown. No person walked along the dark town's sidewalks; an Old West ghost town. The Jeep stopped at a red light.

"Look at the mural on the side of that brick wall," Chris said.

Ben looked. The rudimentary painting depicted a dead man on the sidewalk. The bold caption read "Butte: America's Meth Capitol".

The stoplight turned green and the Jeep crawled forward in search of rest.

# CHAPTER 5

The Jeep shifted into second gear as it slowed and rounded the corner into the dark alleyway. It evaded a pothole and narrowly missed a dumpster that was stationed too far from its usual post. The Jeep turned left and breathed lightly as it moved into open space.

"Here it is," Chris said. "The first stop on our journey."

Ben pulled the Jeep into the hotel parking lot and opened his door. Both boys exited the car quickly and stretched their legs, which were stiff from hours of immobility.

The exterior of the hotel looked weathered; upkeep lacked priority for decades. The architecture told the boys that it was once the finest hotel in the Wild West. Those golden era days passed; Butte was no longer the mining powerhouse of the western frontier, though, judging by the murals, lawlessness still prevailed.

"Let's take all of our bags in with us," Ben suggested, looking cautiously into the dim parking lot.

"But I have so many bags and heavy trunks," Chris said. "Do you think the bellhop will do it for us?"

"By the looks of this town, I doubt this hotel has a bellhop," Ben said.

Ben threw his backpack over his shoulders, while Chris struggled with his trunks. Ben found a wheeled cart and the boys placed Chris' luggage into the platform.

Chris rolled his cart into the hotel and paused at the front desk. He rang the desk bell. Ben looked around and noticed that the Great West Hotel lobby emitted a saloon ambiance.

A middle-aged woman emerged from the back office and approached the front desk. She looked plain, but her eyes were kind. She smiled at Chris.

"Hello, gentlemen," she said. "My name is Michelle. Are you checking in with us this evening?"

"Hi, Michelle," Chris said. "We are checking in."

Michelle processed the reservation and Chris paid with his Wall Street employer's credit card. She handed two room keys to Chris, and the boys strolled to the elevator. They exited on the fifth floor, which was the highest level in the building. Chris opened the door to find two small beds, a boxy television set, and a view of downtown Butte. Ben tossed his backpack on the floor by the window and dove onto his bed. Chris claimed the bed near the door.

"I'm glad we made it," Ben murmured through his pillow.

"Me too," Chris said. He opened the miniature refrigerator. "I'm hungry. What should we eat for dinner?"

"Well, we are in Montana. Home on the range. I'll bet we can find a good steak at a cheap price," Ben said.

"Where should we go? I don't feel like wandering aimlessly through downtown Butte," Chris said. "It doesn't look like my kind of city. Actually, I don't think it qualifies as a city."

"Let's ask Michelle at the front desk. She seemed very helpful," Ben said.

Since they aimed for a steakhouse, Ben and Chris changed into more formal attire in comparison to their athletic gear that they wore during their drive. They left their room and took the stairs to the lobby. Michelle sat on a stool behind the front desk. Her eyes lifted from her book, titled *Small Town Love*. She set her book on the counter, removed her reading glasses, and smiled at the approaching gentlemen.

"Is everything in your room as it should be?" Michelle asked.

"The room is great, Michelle," Ben said.

"We came down here to ask your opinion," Chris said. "Where can we eat a delicious Montana steak around here?"

"Nothing too expensive," Ben added.

Michelle thought for a moment. Her eyes widened and she reached for a pen and a notepad, on which she wrote three directions.

"Just take a left out the front door here. You can walk the whole way. It's less than a half-a-mile," Michelle said.

Ben and Chris felt elated at the idea of walking after sitting in the Jeep for eleven hours.

"If you go to this steakhouse, you have to promise me something," Michelle said.

"What?" the boys asked in unison.

"There's a place across the street that two fellas like you

will want to visit," Michelle said. "It's very bright and lively and you'll be attracted to it."

She paused and made purposeful eye contact with Chris, then with Ben.

"Whatever you do," Michelle said, "*do not* go there."

Michelle returned to her stool and opened her book. She waved to the boys as they turned.

"Enjoy your steak, gentlemen," Michelle said as they left.

"Thanks for your help," Ben shouted.

Chris pondered Michelle's warning, as did Ben. Hunger plagued their stomachs and it increased with each step.

"That was weird," Chris said. "I've had a concierge give me a warning along with a recommendation."

"I've never stayed in a hotel with a concierge," Ben said.

"I wonder what this place is like," Chris said. "How crazy can this place be? This mysterious place that we're not allowed to visit."

"Maybe it's a country place and Michelle doesn't think city boys like us with enjoy it," Ben suggested.

"I wonder if it's owned by the hotel's competitor," Chris said, "and Michelle only wants us to spend money in the Great West Hotel's steakhouse."

Ben and Chris took turns with theories about the forbidden location for the entire half-mile walk, until the drive to eat began to outweigh the drive to think critically.

They reached the steakhouse, which appeared to stand in the center of Old Town Butte. Ben noticed a date emblazoned on the entrance's stone archway: 1892. Above the date, he saw a weathered "Bank of the Frontier" etched into the masonry.

The boys climbed the staircase and sat at the table near

the window. To Ben's left, he noticed and old bank vault. It was open and, inside the vault, two tables awaited impending customers. Chris read from the menu's front page, which included a paragraph about the restaurant's history as a premier bank of the Wild West that was robbed three times before it closed in 1952. In 1976, the decaying, vacant bank was purchased and converted into "the best steakhouse in Montana".

A waitress attended their table immediately, as the dinner rush ended hours ago. Only two other tables were occupied. The night neared its end.

"What can I get you two fine gentlemen to drink?" the waitress asked.

"I'll have a whiskey on the rocks," Chris said. "Not well whiskey. I want the good stuff, please."

Chris took full advantage of his new firm's generosity.

"I'll have your most popular Montana beer, please," Ben said.

"And are we ready to order some dinner?" the waitress said.

Ben and Chris ordered steak and baked potatoes, which the waitress deemed "a real Montana meal." The food arrived and the boys ate their meals in silence, both too hungry to focus on conversation. Car snacks kept hunger just out of reach, but two 22-year-old men needed a full meal to continue their normal interactions. Whether chemically or emotionally, the drinks added looseness to their demeanors.

Chris looked out the window and noticed a mass of motorcycles begin to form. He watched as no less than 75 bikes filled every inch of parking space outside of the establishment across the street. This establishment had neon-pink lights outside, but no windows or signs to indicate the name of the place.

"Hey, Ben," Chris said. "Check this place out. Do you think it's some local biker bar?"

"Looks like it," Ben said. "Judging by the number of Harley-Davidsons parked outside, it looks like a popular spot."

"Let's pay for our dinner and grab a drink over there," Chris suggested.

"Sounds good," Ben said.

Chris paid for both meals; rather, Wall Street's JP Morgan Chase paid for the steaks and the drinks. The boys thanked their waitress and left the old bank.

The evening air in early-summer Montana warmed Ben, or perhaps it was the Butte Pale Ale. The boys crossed the street and squeezed between two old black motorcycles to reach the opposite sidewalk.

"Hey, Chris," Ben said. "Do you think this is the place that Michelle warned us about?"

"This place? No way. Look how popular it is. The whole town is here," Chris said.

Ben knew that Michelle had warned them of this location. He hesitated, but Chris strolled toward the front door with such purpose that Ben followed as if pushed by instinct.

Chris walked to the front door and held it for Ben. The boys crossed the entrance threshold and waited for their eyes to adjust to the dim light. A wooden bar stretched across the entire length of the wood-paneled room. Dingy pool tables and short bar tables filled the room. Leather-

and-denim-clad people occupied every table and barstool.

Ben and Chris maneuvered through the crowd. Every man in the bar had a moustache or sideburns, if not a full beard. Some wore sunglasses, regardless of the low lighting. Some chose to wear their leather jackets, while others exposed their skull-and-crossboned sleeveless shirts. Most jeans possessed holes; some faces had tattoos. Women wore bandanas and clung to their men, though most women in the bar could fight any male counterpart and compete.

Chris puffed his chest and tilted his chin upwards with a tone of superiority. He was not used to mingling with this crowd's socioeconomic status. Ben followed, hands in his pockets. Though the counter space at the bar was full, Chris edged his way between two thick, grizzled men. One looked down at Chris; the man's missing teeth matched the number of remaining yellowed ones, though they hid behind his scowl and moustache.

In his lavender button-up shirt, Chris waved to the bartender and she pointed toward him.

"What'll it be, hun?" she shouted.

"An old fashioned, please," Chris said. "With an extra orange peel."

The bartender narrowed her eyes and stared at Chris. In this bar, a ritzy drink order was rarely made. The bartender started to speak, but Ben interrupted, seeing a confrontational situation brewing.

"And a beer for me, please," Ben shouted.

The bartender poured Ben's beer first and then worked on Chris' cocktail. Her choppy, heavy approach to the cocktail's creation lacked the usual finesse that Chris was accustomed to seeing, but he decided to accept the effort.

The bartender handed the old fashioned to Chris, who sipped it and contorted his face due to the high whiskey proportion.

The boys paid the bartender, again using Chris' Wall Street money. They moved to a section of open wall space by a pool table where two burly men neared the end of a game.

"Let's play some pool," Chris said.

"Do you see an open table?" Ben asked.

They stood on their toes for a better view, but all the tables remained occupied. Chris approached one of the men playing pool next to him.

"Excuse me, sir," Chris said. "We'll take over this pool table when you're done. If you don't mind, of course."

The man strolled confidently toward Chris. His fully tattooed arms gripped the pool stick. He smiled viciously and his goatee curled. The man removed his sunglasses, which revealed the tear-dropped tattoos underneath his eye, along with scars that resembled knife lines.

"You'll have our table, huh?" the man said. "Sorry, but we're using it all night."

His gruff voice punched Chris with physical intimidation; however, Chris was unfamiliar with denial.

"When you're done with this game, we'll pay for the table. All we want is one game," Chris said.

"Well, I'm telling you that you can't have it," the man said.

His opponent finished his shot and joined the scar-faced man. The opponent was short and wiry with piercings on his eyebrows and chin.

"Hey, Scorch," the wiry man said to his scar-faced friend,

"what if he plays the winner of our game?"

The wiry man winked at Scorch, whose face brightened. He stared at Chris.

"You or your buddy will play the winner of our game," Scorch said. "Winner takes 50 bucks from the loser."

"Only 50, eh?" Chris said. "Let's make it 100."

"Deal, you uptown yuppie," Scorch said.

Scorch and Wiry Man finished their game, which Scorch won.

"Ben," Chris said, "I'm not good at pool, but we can't back down from these trailer trash goons. You should play."

"I can't afford to lose 100 dollars. You know that," Ben said. "Why'd you take this bet?"

"Don't worry, Benny. I've got you covered. If Wall Street won't pay for it, then my parents will," Chris said.

"I can't lose your parents money either," Ben said.

"I do it all the time. Besides, in three months, 100 dollars will be nothing to me," Chris said. "Play that poor bastard and let's take his money and have some fun."

"If you insist," Ben said. "It's about time I put my college billiards class to good use."

Ben walked cautiously to the wall and selected a pool cue with an adequate felt tip, which he chalked for ideal game play, or to calm his nerves. Wiry Man returned from the bar with three fellow bikers. All of their jackets had the same oversized patch on the back: crossed shotguns with a skull at the center, surrounded by *Madness Marauders* stitched in bold white letters.

Scorch shot first and pocketed a solid off the break. His second shot missed the corner pocket by a fraction, which provoked the small Madness Marauders crowd. Ben's first shot proved successful, as he knocked a stripe into a side pocket. He scored his follow-up shot, but missed his third, which gave Scorch the table. Again, this provoked cheers from the Madness Marauders, whose crowd had doubled.

Chris finished his old fashioned, so he ordered another, along with a second beer for Ben. Scorch looked at the orange peel in Chris' drink and laughed.

"That's a cute fruit cup you have there," Scorch said.

"This is a highly dignified whiskey cocktail," Chris said.

"Makes you look like a fruit cup," Scorch said. "So does that purple shirt."

The growing group of Madness Marauders roared, which evoked a smile from Scorch. Not to be outdone in a battle of wits with a less educated member of a lower social class, Chris retaliated.

"By the looks of things, you've never been able to afford a drink of this distinction, or a shirt from this designer," Chris said.

The Madness Marauders howled. Scorch threw his head on the pool table and laughed, then threw his head back in hyperbole.

"I missed my last shot," Ben interrupted, strategically. "You're turn."

Scorch breathed heavily in order to refocus his attention to the pool table. Ben stepped back and sipped his beer. He eyed the table. Ben only had two stripes left on the table and both sat near the same corner pocket, while the eight ball rested on the other side of the table. Ben formulated his plan for victory, assuming Scorch missed any of his remaining four solids.

Eventually Scorch missed and left two solids on the

table. The 25 Madness Marauders groaned. Some took shots of whiskey; they had placed drinking bets on every shot. Ben chalked his pool stick and approached the table. He knocked his first stripe into the corner pocket and the cue ball's spin retracted it, which left Ben with an ideal shot for his last stripe. He breathed in, held his breath to steady his hand, and sunk the last stripe into the corner.

"And that just leaves him to sink the eight ball!" Chris shouted to Scorch.

"Quiet down, Chris," Ben said.

"Come on, Ben! You're destroying him!" Chris shouted.

"But I haven't won yet," Ben warned.

Ben walked to the other side of the table to where he sent the cue ball on the last shot. He pointed to the corner pocket and allowed Scorch to witness his anticipated plan. Scorch grinded his teeth and twisted his pool cue in his hands, furious at his impending loss. Ben lined up his pool stick and hit the cue ball cleanly. It ricocheted off of the eight ball, which sunk into the corner pocket, according to plan.

"You won!" Chris shouted.

"No he didn't," Scorch bellowed. "That last shot was a double hit. He hit the cue ball twice."

"No I didn't," Ben said calmly. "My last shot was clean."

"It was a double hit! I saw it!" Wiry Man shouted.

"Yeah, it was double hit!" shouted another Madness Marauder.

Five Madness Marauders stood and gathered around Scorch. Chris stepped forward to offer Ben support.

"I'm telling you, sir, that it was a clean hit," Ben said.

"I'm not giving 100 bucks to a cheater," Scorch said.

"I didn't cheat," Ben said, his temper simmering.

"Well, you've got 25 people here who say you cheated," Wiry Man said.

Ben looked at Chris, who still held his old fashioned. The ice produced dew on the outside of the glass. Ben decided to concede his pride because he recognized a violent situation brewing as a result of clashing egos.

"That's fine," Ben said. "I don't even want your money. Good game, sir. We'll be on our way."

"That's right, you'll be on your way," Scorch said. "After you pay me the 100 dollars you owe me for cheating in our bar."

Chris looked at Ben with an expression of wild concern, fueled by whiskey, which induced false confidence and lack of judgement.

"Listen," Chris said to Scorch. "I know you're trying to hustle us out of our money. You could never pay us the 100 dollars because you're too damn poor. We shouldn't have agreed to play with you white trash bar rats."

More Madness Marauders stood. Some wielded pool sticks, while others fished their pockets for knives. Ben's eyes darted from person to person. His adrenaline heightened his senses.

"What did you call me?" Scorch asked.

"Lesson learned. Never play a gentleman's game with someone who can't spell *gentleman*," Chris said.

Scorch took two steps forward and punched Chris in the stomach with a follow-up punch to Chris' ribs. Wiry Man stepped and pushed Chris with both hands. Scorch wound up for another punch, but Ben kicked him in the stomach.

The entire Madness Marauders gang stood; Ben looked

around the bar in a daze and realized that almost every bar customer belonged to the gang. Terrified, Ben swung his pool stick into Scorch's face, causing him to bleed. Ben reached for a ball on the pool table and threw it at Wiry Man, who collapsed to the floor and clutched his nose in pain.

The Madness Marauders continued their forward surge, eager to destroy the city boys in collared shirts who defamed Scorch. Ben corralled Chris and they sprinted to the door. They burst through the entrance and into the street. As they turned to face their pursuers, the gang stopped at the door. Their immunity ended outside their bar.

Scorch watched intently as Ben and Chris walked toward the Great West Hotel. Ben supported Chris, who still gasped from his punch to the stomach. Ben glanced behind him and saw Scorch smirk.

○   ○   ○

Ben pushed the front door of the hotel and entered the saloon-style lobby. Chris followed. He projected strength, but felt broken. Michelle sat on her stool behind the counter. She placed her book on the table and stood to greet the boys.

"How'd you like your steak?" she asked.

"It was great, thanks," Ben said.

Ben and Chris continued their walk to the elevator in an attempt to avoid the imminent question from Michelle. Both boys felt guilty for failing to uphold their promise.

"You boys didn't go to the biker bar across the street, did you?" Michelle said.

"No, ma'am," Chris lied.

"Good. Enjoy your evening, gentlemen. Let me know if there's anything else you need," Michelle said.

She smiled knowingly and returned to her stool and opened *Small Town Love*. The elevator door opened and the boys rode it to the fifth floor in silence. Ben opened the hotel room door anxiously. Chris entered and crashed onto his bed.

"Thanks for fighting for me, Benny," Chris said.

"Any time," Ben said.

"I shouldn't have said all that stuff to Scarface," Chris said.

"Probably not, but we made it to the hotel safely," Ben said.

Ben thought about Scorch's eerie smile as they left the bar. He neglected to tell Chris about his worries. Still, the smile haunted him. Ben pulled out his journal and pen from his backpack and recorded the evening's events.

"Why are you writing right now?" Chris asked.

"I need to release my creative energy," Ben said.

"Let's get some sleep. We have to wake up early and we have a 12-hour drive tomorrow," Chris said.

"I'll fall asleep soon. Writing before bed calms me down and makes me happy," Ben said.

"No one is ever going to read that journal, you know," Chris said.

"Probably not," Ben said. "I just want to leave my story behind, just in case. I just want to leave behind something more than unused money."

"When you die, the amount of money you leave behind determines how successful you were in life," Chris said.

"Everybody knows that."

"I don't want to be like everybody else. I don't think you can quantify the quality of someone's life based on the sum of unused money in their bank accounts. If someone has a huge bank account left over when they die, that means they weren't generous enough in life. That means they didn't have enough fun," Ben said.

He heard Chris snore from across the room. Ben smiled and returned to his journal.

# CHAPTER 6

Ben's phone alarm sounded, so he rolled to the side of his bed to silence the noise. He heard Chris grumble from the other bed. Chris sat upright and winced as he held his ribcage.

"Damn. That scar-faced biker sure hit me hard in the ribs last night," Chris said.

Chris stood and lifted his shirt, which revealed a black-and-blue, fist-sized circle. Ben chuckled. The boys recalled the events of the prior evening. They laughed at the ridiculous situation in which they found themselves and expressed gratitude for exiting the bar without serious injury. It was a situation which required laughter afterwards to lessen the impact.

Still, Ben felt a sense of foreboding. He recalled Scorch's glare, an image that emblazoned itself into Ben's mind.

Subconsciously, Ben grasped his Saint Christopher medal, which he had not removed since he left Oregon.

Ben grew up with staunch Roman Catholic parents who

took him to church every Sunday morning. He was baptized shortly after birth, received his First Holy Communion in the second grade, and attended confession twice each year. Voluntarily, he decided to proceed through Confirmation, which he completed.

When Ben reached high school, his church attendance dwindled to once per month. Both his mother and father believed wholeheartedly in the Catholic faith and tradition, but when Ben's father was killed during America's War on Terror, Ben's faith in God and the Catholic community faded quickly, almost instantly. When his father died, Ben placed his beloved Saint Christopher medal in a drawer. Six years later, Ben felt unsure about the medal's presence around his neck, but it somehow gave him a sense of security along his American journey.

"Let's get going," Chris said, partly as motivation to himself. "I'll shower first."

Ben looked out the window. *A sunny Montana morning*, he thought. As he had done every morning since age 14, Ben laid on the floor and conducted 200 push-ups, 700 sit-ups, and 50 squats. Years of repetition allowed Ben to conduct his exercises quickly. He reached into his backpack and grabbed his foldable pull-up bar, locked it into the doorframe, and did 50 pull-ups.

When he finished his routine exercises, he wrote a short poem in his journal and then replaced his life's possessions into his backpack as Chris exited the bathroom.

"You're turn," Chris said.

Ben turned on the shower and the water stung his neck, making him wince. When he was done, he checked his neck in the mirror and realized that he had been scratched during the night's bar fight.

"Damn," Ben said as he exited the bathroom. "I thought I left the bar without a scratch."

Chris laughed at Ben's intended use of cliché.

"Ready to drive to South Dakota?" Chris said. "Today's a long one. From what I hear, the scenery isn't too exciting, so I apologize to your camera."

"Let's roll," Ben said.

They grabbed their gear and took the elevator downstairs. Ben saw a sign that advertised the Great West Hotel's coffee and egg buffet.

"Excellent! We made it downstairs in time for the free breakfast," Ben said.

"We don't need to eat that hotel garbage," Chris said. "Let's grab some good food in town before we leave. Besides, my firm will pay for it."

"You don't need to spend money all the time, man," Ben said. "Let's just grab some free food. This hotel has healthy options, like fruit and oatmeal. We would eat the same thing at a restaurant."

"I guess you're right. This will save us time," Chris said. "We can order a real breakfast tomorrow morning in Rapid City."

The boys loaded their plates and pockets with yogurt, oatmeal, bananas, and granola bars, along with two cups of coffee each. As they left the hotel, they told the morning concierge to thank Michelle for her help.

The Jeep waited anxiously in its parking spot. Chris unlatched the trunk flap and the Jeep jumped with excitement for the challenging drive that awaited it. Chris loaded his trunks and bags, and then Ben tossed his 55-liter backpack in the back seat and started the engine. The Jeep revved with anticipation. With Ben in the driver's seat and Chris' passenger seat belt buckled, the Jeep left the Great West Hotel.

In order to return to Interstate 90, the boys had to drive through Old Town Butte. Ben rolled the Jeep to a stop and turned left.

"Hey, let's drive by the biker bar and see what it looks like in the daylight," Chris suggested.

"Alright. Grab my camera. I want to document the location of my first bar fight," Ben said.

The bar was three blocks out the Jeep's necessary path. The Jeep halted at a stoplight between the Old Bank Steakhouse and the Madness Marauders' bar. Ben raised his camera from the driver's seat and adjusted the shutter speed and aperture to account for the influx of Montana sunshine. He eyed the front door through his scope and adjusted the focus.

Through his viewfinder, he saw ten motorcycles parked by the curb. He snapped photographs of the bikes, including license plates. He framed the front door with the bar's address in view. Ben began to feel like an undercover journalist.

The bar's front door opened and Ben snapped five quick pictures of the wiry man exiting the bar.

"No," Chris whispered.

Ben put down his camera. Wiry Man stared directly into the Jeep's cockpit. His eyes widened with sudden recognition and he stepped toward the Jeep.

"Go, Ben," Chris whispered.

"The light's still red," Ben said, panicked.

Ben lifted the camera and took one last picture of Wiry Man. He tossed his camera to Chris, shifted into first gear, and turned right. Through the rear view mirror, Ben saw Wiry Man return to the bar. The boys remained silent until they reached Interstate 90.

"That wiry guy from last night. He saw us. He recognized us," Chris said.

"And he saw me taking pictures," Ben said. "He probably thinks we're government agents."

"Drive fast, Benny," Chris said. "Let's get out of Montana."

The Jeep chugged along the inclined road that swirled above Butte, a town that looked barren and desolate from their elevated perspective. Chris photographed a road sign that read *Continental Divide* and, immediately, the road declined. The Jeep exhaled.

"According to our map, we're staying on Interstate 90 all day. We won't leave it until tomorrow when we reach Minneapolis," Chris said.

"Well, I guess it's time to insert *CD Number Two* and learn some more lyrics," Ben said.

They laughed. A hip-hop song about the glorification of money played through the Jeep's cockpit.

"Chris, are you nervous about your new job?" Ben asked. "It is Wall Street, after all. That's where all the world's money seems to be."

"I suppose I'm a bit nervous," Chris admitted.

"Why? Are you afraid of messing up the numbers?" Ben asked.

"No, no. It's not the numbers," Chris said. "This is what I've always dreamed of doing and I've put a lot of pressure on myself to succeed. So have my parents. It's how I was raised, I suppose. I guess that's why I'm nervous."

"What do you mean?" Ben asked.

"Well, I've always had this ambition to make as much money as possible," Chris said. "Obtaining and maintaining wealth and capital is a Morgan family value. I don't want to fail in my pursuit of that ideal lifestyle."

Ben moved the Jeep into the left lane and sped by a slow-moving semi-truck.

"I've never understood that logic," Ben said. "I mean, what's the purpose of having too much money?"

"To buy things, of course," Chris said. "It's human nature. The person with the most money has the most power, and the most powerful man has the most happiness. Ultimately, that's what I want out of life: the most power. Look at the U.S. Presidents. You don't see poor people as presidential candidates, do you? They don't have enough money."

"Good point," Ben said. "So much for a government as an accurate representation of the people."

"Well, you don't want an idiot running for Congress, do you?" Chris asked.

"Who says poor people are idiots?" Ben asked.

With no logical rebuttal, Chris looked through Ben's camera and changed the setting from manual to automatic. He snapped a few photographs of the Big Sky countryside. The wide, rocky landscape accentuated the sky's openness.

"Look at this rustic farm coming up ahead," Ben said. "Take some pictures of it for me, will you?"

Chris captured images of an old green tractor next to a red barn and silo. Paint crumbled from the barn. In the sunlight, the faded paint seemed to transform from red to brown, then back to red. Two cows stood along the farm's decrepit fence, which was lined with golden field grass and recently cultivated farmland.

"These farmers need an upgrade," Chris said.

"This is an image of Americana, Chris," Ben said. "That's what this road trip has been: a lens into Americana."

"Poor, backwoods Americana," Chris said. "They should sell their land and move to a city. Or buy some paint and make their barn appear a little more respectable."

"Look at these fields," Ben said. "I'll bet these people make a fortune and they don't care what image they portray to people like us who pass by on the highway."

"Everyone upholds and image," Chris said. "No one is ever who they appear to be. We live in a culture based on projected images. Even *reality TV* is scripted. People love it, the fake projection of reality. That's why I want to make money, Benny, so I can afford to project an image of power."

"I don't care what image I project," Ben said. "I just want to be happy."

Chris fished through the limited music options in the glovebox and selected *CD Number Three*. This album included Ben's favorite reggae and peace music selections.

"You need money to be happy, Ben," Chris said. "How are you going to make it in New York without any money?"

Ben pondered the question as he gazed at the vast Montana wilderness. He had achieved happiness throughout his life without much money. Like the farmers that the Jeep passed, Ben's parents had little money, which prompted Ben's father to join the military.

"Of course I need money to survive in New York," Ben said, "but I don't require excess. I just need enough to live."

Chris shrugged in acknowledgement of Ben's ideological differences.

"Seriously, though. What is your plan once we reach New York?" Chris asked.

"I'll become a professional poker player, I suppose," Ben said.

"*Seriously*, Benny. What's your plan?" Chris asked.

"Well, I'll probably find a job as a restaurant server or bartender for a while so I can afford rent and food," Ben said.

"Ultimately, though, what do you want to do?" Chris asked.

"I don't really know," Ben said. "My degree in journalism would make me a good fit for a public relations firm. I know they have some in New York. But I want to be creative. Maybe become an author, or a photographer. Anything that allows me to explore new places. That makes me happy."

"What do you mean?" Chris asked.

"Take this drive, for example," Ben said. "I have almost no money to my name and no secure plan for the future, but seeing America, places I've never seen, this makes me happy. And when I write about it and photograph it, I cement these moments of exploration through creativity, which amplifies my happiness."

"Maybe you can channel those sources of happiness into some actual revenue when we reach the Big Apple," Chris said.

"Maybe," Ben said.

A soft reggae song played through the stereo. Chris leaned against the door; his eyes flickered in an attempt to fight sleep. The rhythm of the beat and the rumble of the road allowed sleep to win. As Chris napped, Ben listened to the next song that played on *CD Number Three*.

*Don't need no money,*
*Don't need no fame.*
*Only love and happiness,*
*Rule this game.*

The ukulele riff lasted for one minute. Ben vowed to learn this song on the ukulele once he reached New York. If nothing else, he could play music on the street corner for money. He lacked practice on his ukulele, which he had played sporadically since the fourth grade. Ben looked out the side window. Family farms blurred with the landscape. *Don't need no mo-ney…*

○    ○    ○

Chris awoke as the Jeep stopped. He spun left and right frantically as he acquired his bearings. Chris looked to the driver's seat, which was empty. A brief sense of panic overcame him. He felt his pulse quicken and a bead of sweat formed on his forehead.

He spun around and, through the window, he saw Ben filling the gas tank. With aching knee joints, Chris exited the Jeep and stretched. He paced around the Jeep and noticed two motorcycles sitting in the opposing fueling station.

"Where are we?" Chris asked.

"Billings, Montana," Ben said. "You slept for a while, there, sunshine."

"I couldn't fight it," Chris said.

The boys laughed. The sun hung high in the air and scorched the pavement. The baked, desert environment reminded Ben of the Western movies that he used to watch as a kid with his dad on his family's boxed television.

Chris strolled away from the Jeep and entered the small shop that accompanied the gas station. He walked stiffly to the coffee spout and poured one cup for himself and another for Ben. He placed travel lids on the paper cups and stood in line behind two men who purchased chewing tobacco and cigarillos.

Both men wore weathered black shirts with cut-off sleeves, which exposed their fully tattooed arms. One man wore a motorcycle helmet without a visor; the other man wore a pirate-like bandana. The bandana-clad man sported a full moustache. As the man raised his arm to the clerk to grab his chewing tobacco, Chris noticed a familiar symbol tattooed on his arm: crossed shotguns with a skull at the center.

"I wish we could afford another can of chew," the bandana man to his compatriot. "I go through this stuff real quick."

The men left and Chris paid for the two cups of coffee. Since his hands were full, he used his foot to push the door open and he walked toward the Jeep.

Ben returned the fuel nozzle to its holster. At the opposing fuel station, the two men sat on their motorcycles. One placed sunglasses over his eyes, while the other man paused and eyed the Jeep. His eyes focused on the license plate, and then he lifted his head toward the boys.

"Where you Massachusetts boys goin'?" the bandana man said.

Ben and Chris looked at each other for reassurance.

"We're leaving Montana for the East Coast," Chris said.

"Just passing through," Ben added.

The man nodded slowly. He placed his sunglasses on his face and dropped his hand, starting his motorcycle. His helmeted counterpart did the same. The bandana man watched as Chris jumped into the driver's seat.

The Jeep left the gas station quickly. Chris looked into the rear view mirror and saw the bandana man place a cellphone to his ear. His head followed the Jeep as it returned to Interstate 90.

"I think I found our boys," the bandana man said into his phone.

"Follow 'em," Scorch said from the other end.

Two motorcycle engines roared and sped onto Interstate 90, heading east.

# CHAPTER 7

Chris piloted the Jeep as it cruised down Interstate 90. The sun hung in the air, giving the impression of the Wild West at high noon. A train sped west, running parallel to the highway; since it travelled the opposite direction as the Jeep, the train appeared to move twice as fast due to relative motion. Ben expected to witness a train robbery by bandits on horseback, but he knew this was a foolish thought. Still, his childlike imagination hoped it would happen. Again, he recalled the television Westerns that he watched as child with his father.

Ben pulled out the paper map, which was losing its pristine flatness. Some of the edges curled. He unfolded it and mapped the Jeep's trajectory.

"Hey, Chris, you know about General Custer, right?" Ben asked.

"A little," Chris said. "Why?"

"On the map, it shows that we're close to Custer National Forest," Ben said. "Do you think that's where the

Battle of Little Bighorn happened?"

"You tell me, history major," Chris said.

Ben traced the line from Billings to Custer National Forest. He squinted his eyes to see the small font that indicated the offshoot highway's number.

"It doesn't look too far away," Ben said. "If we take Highway 212 instead of Interstate 90, it should take us through Custer National Park and bring us out close to Rapid City."

Chris thought for a moment. He had planned his route perfectly based on time, speed, and gas efficiency, but he neglected to plan for detours and sightseeing. He weighed the advantages and disadvantages of this particular detour before he came to his final decision.

"Alright, navigator," Chris said. "Where do I turn?"

"The junction should come soon," Ben said.

After 30 miles, Ben began to doubt the existence of Highway 212. Realistically, he thought that the Jeep had passed the junction already and did not realize it.

"Highway 212, right?" Chris asked.

"Yes, sir," Ben said.

"Here it is," Chris said, with partial disbelief.

The Jeep veered onto its new route, which required a slower speed based on the nature of the road. Soon, Ben photographed the *Custer National Forest* sign and the Jeep pulled into a crowded parking lot. Based on the crowd, the boys assumed they landed at the visitor center.

A few herculean RVs sat in the oversized parking spots at the entrance to the lot, while station wagons and motorcycles filled the remaining vacancies. Families roamed the visitor center cement space. Overweight mothers with visors and fanny packs ushered small, bored children who wanted to play handheld video games rather than appreciate the opportunity for history and family bonding.

Ben and Chris wandered away from the visitor center crowds and followed a dirt path that wound through dry grass. They were the only hikers on the trail. Chris hesitated when they came to a rattlesnake warning sign, but Ben continued, so Chris followed, not wanting to appear cowardly. Plus, he trusted Ben's hiking and backpacking experience.

The boys weaved through the knee-high brush on the dirt path until they came to a monument. A forest ranger in a green shirt and wide-brimmed hat stood alone by the monolith. He appeared middle-aged with a round belly and a white, whiskered face that peeled slightly from constant sun exposure.

"Welcome, gentlemen," the forest ranger said. "How are you doing on this hot afternoon?"

"We're doing well, sir. How are you?" Ben said.

"I'm just fine," the ranger said. "Is this your first time here?"

"It is," Ben said.

"Well isn't that great? Would you like me to tell you what you're looking at?" the ranger asked.

"Sure," Chris said.

The ranger dove into his well-rehearsed story of the history of Little Bighorn. He explained that during the late 1800s, the U.S. government wanted to expand its territory, but the Native Americans to the west disagreed with this idea because they lived on the land. The U.S. government dispatched a battalion to dispose of the Native American tribes and heard them onto reservations.

The Lakota people lived in the area that surround the Little Bighorn River. The ranger pointed ahead so the boys could see the river for themselves.

He continued, saying that General Custer and his troops approached the Lakota people and asked them to leave the land. The Lakota people declined, so a battle commenced. All of the Lakota women and children were down by the river when General Custer's battalion invaded; the battalion slaughtered many women and children. The Lakota warriors fought off General Custer's forces and shot Custer dead with an onslaught of arrows.

"This monument before us, gentlemen, is the grave of the great General Custer," the ranger said.

Ben photographed the grave. As he took the photo, his thoughts replayed the ranger's last comment. Before Ben had a chance to speak, Chris voiced his opinion.

"The *great* General Custer?" Chris asked. "Didn't you just say that he slaughtered women and children?"

The forest ranger attempted to hide his panic.

"Yes, but it was in the defense of our great nation," the ranger said.

"And what, exactly, was Custer defending?" Chris asked.

"The land that rightfully belonged to the United States, of course," the ranger said.

"Are you sure?" Ben asked.

"Of course," said the ranger.

"You're wrong, sir," Ben said. "The Lakota people lived on this land for centuries. The U.S. government actually signed peace and land treaties with Lakota, which guaranteed the land rights to the Lakota people, but the U.S.

government wanted the land for their own greed and glory. They wanted this land so much that they were willing to break their treaties and slaughter hundreds of thousands of native people in order to gain a profit."

"But the Lakota people killed General Custer and won the Battle of Little Bighorn," the ranger said. "They were the real winners."

"Did the Lakota win?" Ben asked. "Tell me, where are the Lakota people now? I don't see any around."

"Well, they moved to the reservations given to them by our gracious government," the ranger said.

Ben fumed. Even Chris, who cherished the value of profit, simmered at the glorification of slaughter.

"Have you been to an Indian Reservation?" Ben asked. "They are the most unusable, unwanted pieces of land in the world. No one would choose to live there, given a fair choice instead of the end of a gun barrel."

The ranger removed his hat and wiped sweat from his brow. Though the heat made him perspire, this sweat came from nerves and confrontational adrenaline.

"Did you do any of this research on your own, or did you just recite the guidebook that the U.S. government spoon-fed to you when they offered you this job?" Ben asked.

"Let's move along, Benny," Chris said. "Let's see where the next trail leads."

Ben glared at the forest ranger until Chris physically turned him away. The boys walked briskly onto another trail until the hills and tall straw grass blocked Custer's grave from view. The trail wound into a small valley.

Ben fumed and Chris could see his friend's expressive

outrage.

"That idiot," Ben said. "He doesn't understand that U.S. pride killed the Native American culture and way of life."

"He's just a blind, proud American," Chris said. "Don't let it get to you. Besides, the U.S. government doesn't do that stuff anymore."

Ben exhaled forcefully.

"You know, Chris, I think they do," Ben said.

"How so?" Chris asked.

"Why did the United State military invade Iraq?" Ben asked.

"To fight terrorism and get revenge on the guys who bombed the World Trade Center on September Eleventh," Chris said.

"That's what the media told us," Ben said. "The people who bombed the Twin Towers weren't even hiding in Iraq. They hid in Afghanistan, which is why we invaded that country."

"Good point," Chris said. "So, why did we invade Iraq?"

"Oil," Ben said. "The U.S. military invaded Iraq to control oil imports and exports coming out of the Middle East. Remember when gas prices doubled after Nine-Eleven? The U.S. government is controlled by the money, not by altruism."

"What do you mean?" Chris said?

"George W. Bush, the President at the time of the U.S. invasion of Iraq, used to lead a major oil company before he became the commander in chief. That's where he got all his money to run for President, not to mention his father's former presidential status. President Bush used the power of fear within the American people to make them believe that an attack on Iraq would make us safer at home, when all he wanted to do was jack up the oil prices and make the U.S. economy stronger, along with his old oil buddies who donated to his presidential campaign," Ben said.

"I guess I never thought about it like that," Chris said.

"Neither did my dad," Ben said. "Or maybe he did, but couldn't do anything about it since he was a government soldier. A pawn in George Bush's game."

Ben looked across the dry, grassy plain. He focused on the Little Bighorn River and imagined gunshots and arrows and women screaming to save their small, helpless children. Rage boiled inside of him for the past. And the present. His mind worked furiously.

"It's the same thing Western culture has done for centuries," Ben continued. "In the Christian Crusades, religious leaders sent waves of military forces to Muslim-occupied Jerusalem to steal treasures and expand their Christian Empire. All in the name of God. Christians forget about the Crusades, you know. That's why they repeat the Crusades by invading Iraq and stealing the treasures of the Muslims. Only now, that treasure is oil instead of gold and sacred relics."

Ben breathed heavily and continued.

"All these so-called Christians are always the first ones to judge others for their differences, always the first to persecute, always in the name of God. They're the real false prophets," Ben said.

Chris said nothing. He allowed Ben to work through his anger. Chris rarely saw Ben's temper flare, so he let Ben continue his rant. Though Ben spouted on in anger toward the ranger, the U.S. military, and Christian religious institutions, Chris knew the root cause of Ben's frustrations came from the open wound of his father's death, a wound that Ben had never fully closed.

They continued their stroll until it led to another clearing. The circular space featured Native American-inspired horse sculptures crafted from bronze. According to a plaque, this hidden area of the park was newly created by local Native American tribal councils.

Between the horse statues, Ben read inspirational quotations by famous Native American leaders who spoke about peace and forgiveness.

"I doubt the forest rangers make it to this part of the park," Chris said.

"Peace and forgiveness," Ben said. "What a novel concept."

o     o     o

The boys returned to the Jeep and sped along Highway 212. Chris knew that the detour to Little Bighorn possessed an intangible value for his personal intellect, but he felt a need to return to his carefully planned itinerary and make up for lost time.

Ben's temper fizzled in the car as he looked at the map. He embraced his new role as navigator. With his index finger, Ben tracked the mileage from the Highway 212 junction to Rapid City, South Dakota.

Ben snapped a photograph of the *Welcome to Wyoming* road sign. Immediately after entering Wyoming, the roads produced a red tint. Barbed wire fences lined the highway and rolling hills of grass faded behind them. Dusk approached, but sunlight beat down on the prairie. Chris looked to his right and noticed a sign that warned against deer crossing the road. He saw the barbed wire fences and thought nothing of the warning.

"Hey, Ben," Chris said, "We have a half tank left, but would you mind if we stop for gas now?"

"Sure," Ben said. "Why?"

"Have you heard of a town called Sturgis?" Chris asked.

"Yeah," Ben said.

"Look on the map," Chris said. "Will we pass through it before we reach Rapid City?"

"Yeah," Ben said. "Who cares?"

Chris slouched his head in preparation to divulge his fear and deflate his pride.

"I hear Sturgis is a wild motorcycle town," he said. "Every summer, the town holds a massive motorcycle rally and thousands of bikers show up. I've never thought about it until we saw those motorcycle riders at the gas station in Billings. One of them had a tattoo of that same Madness Marauders symbol. I just don't want to run into that scar-faced guy again."

Chris braced himself for Ben's response to his admission of weakness.

"I understand," Ben said. "Let's fill up before we hit Sturgis. That's a smart idea."

"Great," Chris said as he looked toward Ben.

Then, Chris saw it. The impending danger coiled on the roadside in an athletic stance. The four-pronged deer had scaled the barbed wire fence and waited in the emergency lane and watched the Jeep cruise down the highway.

The Jeep prepared to make an evasive maneuver. Chris'

nerves fired through his entire body. Adrenaline pumped through his hands.

Finally, Chris and the deer made eye contact. Then, the deer bounded forward onto the road.

The Jeep aimed directly for the deer's center. Chris shifted into fourth gear, honked his horn, and then jammed his foot into the brake pedal. The deer glanced toward the Jeep's snarling grill while it darted across the asphalt. The boys braced for impact, but the Jeep slowed enough for the deer to pass safely.

Chris' heart thumped audibly. Ben held his breath and could not exhale. Fear coursed through the Jeep's cockpit. The near-miss left the boys silent for an eternity.

"Great driving, Chris," Ben said.

Chris remained silent. His eyes focused on the road.

Finally, the Jeep crossed into South Dakota territory. The Jeep passed a road sign that indicated that Sturgis was 27 miles ahead. The boys looked for gas station advertisements and pulled off the highway into a town called Whitewood.

Chris realized that he had stopped closer to Sturgis than he originally planned, so he filled the gas tank quickly and returned to the driver's seat.

The Jeep accelerated onto the highway and merged in front of a single motorcycle. The motorcycle driver wanted to move faster, so he sped around the Jeep.

Chris looked at the driver and recognized him as the helmeted man from the Billings gas station. The driver looked at Chris and nodded before he sped into the horizon. Chris did not mention that he recognized the driver.

Abiding by the road sign, Chris slowed the Jeep to 25

miles per hour and rolled through Sturgis. Motorcycle bars overflowed and Harley-Davidsons chopped through the side streets. Leather-clad tourists and rally-goers roamed sidewalks, most with cigarettes in hand.

A four-way stop approached. To the Jeep's left, a line of motorcycles awaited their turn to progress through the legal impediment. The Jeep accelerated forward, followed by three motorcycles.

The speed limit increased to 40 miles per hour, so the Jeep accelerated lightly. The three motorcycles sped in front of the Jeep and slowed, so Chris slowed to keep from crashing. Two more motorcycles approached the Jeep from both sides and drove parallel with it.

Then, four bikes approached from behind, which left the Jeep boxed between two bikes.

"What's going on, Benny?" Chris said with a panic-stricken voice.

Ben looked at the bikers on his side of the Jeep and saw familiar patchwork: crossed shotguns with a skull at the center.

"Chris, I think it's the gang from the bar in Butte," Ben said. "I think it's the Madness Marauders."

"What should I do?" Chris asked.

"Stay calm," Ben said. "Just keep driving forward at their pace. They probably don't even recognize us."

A biker next to Chris made an insulting hand gesture to the Jeep.

"I think they know who we are," Chris said.

"Maybe not," Ben said. "Maybe they just hate four-wheeled vehicles driving through Sturgis."

"Always optimistic," Chris said.

A biker next to Ben raised a wooden baseball bat and signaled for Chris to pull over his car. Though Ben could not hear him, he saw the biker use distinct foul language.

"They want us to pull over," Ben said to Chris. "Don't do it."

"Then what should I do?" Chris said.

"Keep driving," Ben said. "They can't do anything to us while we're driving."

The biker with the baseball bat raised his weapon high above his head. He swung down and cracked his bat on the Jeep's hood. Car paint chips flew and a steel-blue dent formed. Another Madness Marauder emerged and he wielded a metal bar. He swung hard at the same spot on the Jeep's hood, which created a deep dent.

"They're destroying the Jeep!" Chris shouted. "What do we do? What if someone pulls out a gun?"

Chris' knuckles whitened and he lost circulation to his fingers from a tight grip on the steering wheel. His left eye twitched from nervous-system overload.

"Take a deep breathe, buddy," Ben said. "Here's what we're going to do. We'll take it one step at a time. Just follow my directions."

Chris breathed four times, deep and controlled.

"Alright, now I want you to turn on your right turn signal," Ben said. "Slow down to 10 miles per hour and move into the far right lane."

"We're pulling over?" Chris shouted. "Are you crazy? They'll kill us! All over some stupid game of pool."

"Trust me, Chris," Ben said.

"This is all my fault," Chris muttered. "I never should have be so damn disrespectful to those guys. Who cares if they're poor?"

The Jeep slowed and its blinkers indicated its intention to move to into the right lane. The Madness Marauders in the right lane slowed and allowed the Jeep to shift into their spot.

"See this exit coming up?" Ben said. "Take it. Slowly."

"Alright," Chris said hesitantly.

The one-lane exit forced the squadron of motorcycles to fall back behind the Jeep. A stop sign awaited the group at the end of the exit. A crossroad ran underneath the highway and a return ramp to the highway was ahead of the crossroad.

To the left, Ben saw a semi-truck surge forward. Its speed indicated that the semi-truck intended to continue forward on the crossroad, rather than enter the highway.

"We're coming to the stop sign, Benny," Chris said. "If we stop, that gang will have us out of the Jeep in no time."

"Shift into second gear," Ben said.

The stop sign approached. The semi-truck neared the intersection. The Madness Marauders fanned and waited for the Jeep to rest.

"Punch it, Chris!" Ben shouted. "Go!"

The Jeep sprinted forward, passing the stop sign. The semi-truck barreled toward it and braked hard. The Jeep sped through the intersection and reached the highway's on-ramp, while the semi-truck stopped in the middle of the intersection, blocking the motorcycles from pursuing their prey.

Chris accelerated to 80 miles per hour and exhaled, finally. Ben turned and looked out the back window to make sure that the Jeep had no pursuers. Ben shouted.

"We did it!" Ben screamed. "Great driving, yet again, Chris."

"We almost died back there," Chris said. "You're crazy."

"That semi-truck almost smashed us," Ben said.

"What's going to happen when that gang catches up to us again?" Chris asked.

"They can't," Ben said.

"How do you know?" Chris asked.

"We just filled up the gas tank!" Ben shouted. "We can drive for hours without stopping."

The boys laughed. Ben's chuckle sounded confident; Chris' was forced; fear still gripped him.

The Jeep powered along the highway without any indications of slowing down. Chris looked through his side window; fence posts and mile posts blurred together. His eye hunted for deer. He glanced at his rear view mirror and expected to see motorcycles in pursuit, but he saw only the sun begin to set over the plains.

The road faded into the horizon; the Jeep left no tracks. Chris wondered if the Madness Marauders would follow the Jeep into new territory, or if the Jeep was far enough into a new, safe landscape.

# CHAPTER 8

Ben looked at his camera screen and investigated the photograph of the *Welcome to South Dakota* sign that he had taken before nearing Sturgis. He smiled, pleased with the shot. His photography skills improved with every state line that the Jeep crossed. Ben held the camera lens to the window, but his hands still shook from the highway chase, so he returned his camera to its case.

The Jeep's windshield was littered with a variety of insect species, as was the grill, which needed a flossing. The recent dent in the hood gave the Jeep a rugged face and it accelerated with a new, aggressive attitude. It seemed to roar like a motorcycle.

The sun descended as the boys pulled into their hotel in Rapid City. Ben and Chris unloaded their bags and trunks on a rolling cart and brought them to the entrance. Chris checked in using JP Morgan Chase's good graces. He returned to the Jeep and parked his car in a discrete location. Still, Chris reverberated from the encounter with the motorcycle gang.

The hot day's drive, paired with the deer crossing and the motorcycle bashing, left the boys in a state of exhaustion, but they ordered a local, South Dakota beer at the hotel bar before they found their room. As the sun dropped below the horizon, the boys walked out to a grass patio with their beers.

Chris noticed two attractive girls sitting at a table near their own. He motioned for Ben to look in their direction. Ben turned back toward Chris with hesitation.

"Come on, Benny," Chris said. "Go talk to them."

"I can't, man," Ben said.

"Why not?"

Ben looked at Chris with a knowing expression.

"Don't tell me that you won't go talk to them because you're still hung up on Samantha," Chris said. "Benny, you need to get over her. This is the perfect opportunity. Besides, all you have to do is *talk* to them."

Ben glared at Chris, which forced a reaction that Ben dreaded, but slightly anticipated.

Chris stood and walked toward the girls' table and sat down, which left Ben sitting alone awkwardly, so he stood and sat next to Chris at the girls' table, too.

"Hey, guys," said the pretty blonde girl.

"Is it alright if we join you?" Ben asked.

The blonde girl smiled.

"Of course it is," she said. "I'm Lucy. And this is my friend, Mary Anne."

Lucy pointed to her brunette friend at her side.

"I'm Ben, and this is Chris."

Lucy smiled at Mary Anne.

"Well, it's nice to meet you, boys," Lucy said. "What brings you to Rapid City?"

"We're on a road trip to New York," Ben said. "We just graduated from the University of Oregon, so we're headed out there for work."

"We're on a road trip, too!" Mary Anne shouted.

"We're headed to Philly, and then maybe to New York," Lucy said. "We'll see."

"What prompted your road trip?" Chris asked.

"Well, we're students from University of Colorado," Lucy said. "I just graduated and Mary Anne still has one more year. Her family is from a town near Philly, so we're going out there to visit and see where the summer takes us."

Chris gave Ben an encouraging smile.

"Do you have any job plans now that you're graduated?" Ben asked Lucy.

"Not really," she said. "I love to play the violin, but it's difficult to find steady work in Colorado with that skillset. I majored in accounting, but I don't want to sit at a desk all day, you know? I want to get out and experience the world and make it a better place and breathe in all that I can."

Ben stared at Lucy intently.

"You think I'm crazy, don't you?" Lucy said.

"No, actually, I don't," Ben said. "I think that's an incredible outlook."

Lucy smiled and looked up at Ben with adoring eyes, a look which he reciprocated.

After their pint glasses were empty, Ben and Chris stood to leave. Chris was tired, but Ben wanted to continue his conversation with Lucy. He admired her intellect; she spoke about the world and her life with such purpose that it caused Ben to become infatuated.

Ben and Chris took the elevator to their hotel room floor. A sudden wave of exhaustion flooded Chris, while Ben only thought about Lucy.

"Well, are you over Samantha now, lover boy?" Chris said.

"Lucy was amazing, wasn't she?" Ben said.

"Did you get her phone number?" Chris asked.

"No," Ben said. "I'll never see her again."

Chris stood on his bed.

"She's going to Philly and then *maybe* to New York!" Chris shouted. "Go back down there and get her number. You can initiate seeing her again if you're in the same city."

Ben did not hesitate. He dashed through the door and burst onto the elevator. When the elevator reached the bottom floor, he jetted through it before it was fully open. He sprinted through the bar and onto the patio.

He saw two empty pint glasses on the girls' table.

o    o    o

A flash jolted Ben awake. He forgot to close the window shade before he fell asleep, so the early sunrise shot him in the eye. He contemplated shutting the blinds and sleeping for another hour, but he decided to conduct his morning exercise routine instead.

He showered and then wrote in his journal; in this entry, he mapped a rough plan for his own financial survival in New York. His plan included: a part-time bartending job, selling photographs of New York City, and hunting for a major public relations career position. In all, he allowed himself two weeks to find a career. Ben found little confidence in this plan's sustainability, but it was a plan nonetheless.

If this failed, he possessed a backup plan, though he hesitated to use it.

Ben knew that his mother lived in New York, but their relationship had strained when she moved there. As an aspiring Broadway actress, she had limited success and made little money; therefore, she never had a reliable phone number for Ben to call. Ben spoke to his mother once in a while. She called every year on his birthday.

She was unaware of his spontaneous move to the City, and he had no intentions to inform her of his choice because he feared that he would feel obliged to spend time with her. Ben felt that she retreated to a mode of self-preservation after Ben's father died. Ben felt that she had left her son to progress through life on his own. Ultimately, Ben decided to do just that.

Chris awoke with his alarm. He found Ben in a chair by the window as he read *A People's History of the United States*.

"Since when did you become a morning person?" Chris asked.

"About an hour ago," Ben said.

They laughed. Chris showered and dressed in a short timeframe. Ben suggested the hotel's free breakfast bar in order to save money. Chris conceded, only in the interest of saving time. The boys loaded the Jeep. Chris sat in the driver's seat, while Ben looked at the U.S. map in his passenger seat.

"Mount Rushmore looks close to Rapid City," Ben said. "It's out of our way, but it's close."

"I've always wanted to see it," Chris said.

"Me too. It is a famous image of Americana," Ben said.

Chris sipped his free hotel coffee and shifted into first gear. The Jeep pulled away from the hotel and away from Interstate 90. The Mount Rushmore detour drew the Jeep southward.

Trees became dense and the elevation seemed to rise. Rustic mountain cabins hid through the tree line. Chris drove; the highway wound through small towns, different than the small towns along the farmland highway. These small places blended with the mountains. The winding road provided the Jeep with an opportunity to practice its agility, opposed to the forward sprint of the Interstate.

The Jeep found a parking spot once it completed the climb to the National Monument border. Ben and Chris strolled up the staircase and paused.

The boys faced a long concrete entryway, lined with flags from every U.S. state and territory. At the end of the path, in full view, stood Mount Rushmore. Ben and Chris followed the path until they reached the viewing platform.

"Look at the size of those faces," Ben said.

"How did *humans* make this?" Chris asked.

The stone faces of four U.S. presidents looked at the boys.

"They're like those Easter Island heads," Ben said.

"Except we know who made these ones," Chris said.

They laughed.

"Let's check out the visitor center," Chris said. "Maybe I'll buy a souvenir."

They entered the gift shop. Ben laughed at the tacky trinkets that lined the shelves: scale models of Mount

Rushmore, pink snow globes with presidential faces, and postcards with poor graphic design work. Ben never understood the appeal of a postcard, but he had a sudden appreciation for the photographic skill that most postcards portrayed.

Chris roamed the book aisle and looked at titles that alluded to the history of Mount Rushmore's construction. He exited the aisle and walked into an open space. An old man sat in a chair by a table that was full of copies of a single book title. Chris walked closer and read a sign on the table. *Book Signing - Henry Stromwell: Builder of Mount Rushmore.*

"Hey, Ben!" Chris shouted.

Every head in the silent gift shop turned.

"Come here!" Chris shouted again.

Ben walked to him.

"See this old guy in the chair?" Chris whispered. "He was a construction worker on Mount Rushmore. Isn't that wild?"

"No way! He has to be 95 years old. There aren't too many of these guys left," Ben said.

"Let's talk to him," Chris said. "Besides, he looks bored. He's falling asleep in his chair."

Ben looked at the old man. He wore a cap that indicated his World War two veteran status. His leather jacket was oversized, but it fit well during the prime of his life. He hunched from his neck to the middle of his spine. His eyebrows protruded underneath the bill of his hat.

As the boys approached, the old man straightened and projected pride.

"Hello, sir," Ben said.

"Hello, boys," the old man said.

"You helped build Mount Rushmore?" Chris asked, rather bluntly.

The old man smiled. A memory flashed through his mind and lingered.

"You bet I did," he said.

"That's incredible," Chris said.

"Can you tell us about it?" Ben said.

"You should read my book, son," the old man said.

"I wish I could, but I don't have enough money to buy a new book right now," Ben said. "I just graduated from college and I don't have a job yet. But we'd love to hear your story."

The old man pondered. He glanced at his agent, a middle-aged man in a suit, who was speaking with the store manager. The old man smirked, then returned his attention to the boys.

"Well," the old man started, "I started working on the mountain when I was 17 years old. Since I was a young fella, the government suits gave me a fun job: a dangler. They tied ropes to my waist and then I'd jump down and hang in front of the presidents' faces. Then, I would spend all day chiseling away. I did that every day until I turned 20. You see, I was a nose expert."

"A nose expert?" Chris asked.

"Why, yes. I chiseled Thomas Jefferson's nose, most of Washington's, and the bridge of Lincoln's."

"Was it scary?" Chris asked.

"Hanging up there, 300 feet in the air, on those ropes?" the old man said. "Sure it was!"

He slapped his knee and chuckled wheezily.

"But when I turned 20, I sure wasn't afraid of heights

anymore," the old man continued. "I suppose that's why I became a paratrooper in the War."

"You were in World War Two?" Ben asked.

"Yes, sir," the old man said, somberly.

Ben's eyes widened. His mind flipped through potential questions to ask the man. Then, the thought of his own father in war emblazoned itself over Ben's eyes.

"Would you like to hear about it?" the old man asked.

Ben and Chris nodded vigorously.

"Well," the old man began, "I enlisted in the Navy, so they sent me to Hawaii, to a base called Pearl Harbor. It was a nice place, really…"

The man's agent finished his discussion with the store manager and approached rapidly.

"Alright, Henry," the agent said. "These guys need to buy your book if they want to hear your story."

Chris widened his eyes. Ben felt an upsurge of emotion from his soul. Chris stepped toward the agent.

"He was just talking about his life, sir," Chris said. "There's no need to act defensive."

"Gentlemen," the agent said," unless you've purchased Mr. Henry Stromwell's book, I'm going to demand that you move along."

The agent's eyes narrowed. Chris felt confrontational, but Ben spoke first.

"Mr. Stromwell," Ben said, "it was an honor to meet you."

"You as well," the old man said.

The boys exited the visitor center. They felt riled with excitement. Chris wanted to return to the visitor center and confront the agent, but he allowed the thrill of history and storytelling to become an overriding sentiment.

As they walked along the flagged path, with the presidential faces of Mount Rushmore in their wake, Ben felt emotion begin to swell within his core. He was unsure what to name this emotion, but it continued to rise.

A tear escaped his eye, followed by another. Ben leaned against the wall with all of his weight; the Hawaiian flag hung above him and seemed to wave. Tears flowed from his eyes. He slid down the wall and sat on the concrete and buried his face in his knees.

"Ben, what's up?" Chris asked.

Ben held up his hand, indicating that he needed time to wrestle with the emotion on his own. Chris looked around, unsure how to help his friend. Tourists flocked through the flagged pathway. Some noticed Ben's tears, but most passed, unaware of any emotion but their own. Chris focused only on Ben.

"Hey, buddy," Chris said. "Are you alright?"

Ben sniffled and wiped his face with his shirtsleeve.

"Yeah, I'll be alright," Ben said through chokes.

He breathed deeply. In. Out. In. Out.

"Sorry about that," Ben continued.

"What happened?" Chris asked.

Ben thought. He needed time to rationalize his emotion. The combination of the old man's silenced journey through war and the immense power of the stone presidents and the flags of every U.S. territory blowing in the wind swirled together inside of Ben's soul and unleashed an emotion that Ben could only describe as a hurricane.

"I don't know what happened," Ben said. "I experienced a powerful moment."

"That's what Americana does to people," Chris said. "It moves them. It changes them."

The boys declined the staircase and climbed into the Jeep. Without noise, they drove through the forest and returned to Interstate 90.

o   o   o

B en looked at the map, and at the stereo clock, and then back at the map. The detour to Mount Rushmore left them two hours behind schedule. Ben did not mind; he knew that they were in no hurry to reach Minneapolis. Chris' necessity to remain punctual agitated Ben, while Ben's lack of concern for an itinerary bothered Chris.

Ben looked at the map again.

"It looks like we're ten miles from Badlands National Park," Ben said.

"I've heard of the Badlands," Chris said. "What are they?"

"I don't know, but it looks like it's just a short detour off of Interstate 90," Ben said.

"Well, our detour to Mount Rushmore put us way behind schedule," Chris said.

"So, what's another hour?" Ben asked.

"Fair enough. Where do I go from here?" Chris said.

The Jeep exited Interstate 90 and drove onto a road that quickly ushered the boys away from any indication of civilization. The sky turned black with cloud cover. The landscape became flat and desolate. Only prairie brush populated the eternal field that sprawled out the Jeep's window.

"This is weird, Benny," Chris said. "My phone doesn't have service. I don't even see a house or a farm."

Ben looked out the window and internalized his nervousness.

"Are you sure we're going the right direction?" Chris asked.

"Of course," Ben said. ""I'm pretty sure, anyway."

"What if the Jeep breaks down? Who would we call? We can't walk back to the Interstate from here," Chris said.

"We'll be fine," Ben said. "This road has to lead *somewhere*. I think I read the map correctly."

Chris looked at Ben with frustration. His perfectly planned road trip was at risk of destruction because he listened to Ben's whim. *That's why Ben is with me and not working for Portland Public Relations*, Chris thought. *He just flies through life without a sure plan.*

The boys drove in silence. *CD Number Four* played through the stereo, but it was scratched, so the music chopped. Chris turned off the stereo. His knuckles whitened as he drove in silent angst.

Then, they saw it. The unearthly physical features rose from the ground in front of the Jeep. Clay towers, deep canyons. Ben pulled out his camera and photographed a sign: *Welcome to Badlands National Park*.

The Jeep tiptoed forward. The landforms ahead looked foreboding.

"This is wild," Chris said.

"These landforms look like giant ant farms," Ben said.

"I feel like I'm on the Moon," Chris said. "This is the craziest landscape I've ever seen."

The Jeep slowed as it entered the Badlands' formations.

To the left, a steep, never-ending cliff of petrified clay. To the right, a ten-story tower of crumbly earth.

The Jeep weaved cautiously through formations, which seemed to morph with every turn. The unpredictability of the landscape confused Jeep and driver.

"I bet this is how Neil Armstrong felt when he walked on the Moon," Ben said.

"Didn't he hit a golf ball up there?" Chris asked.

"Maybe," Ben said. "That could be a legend."

"I have golf clubs in the Jeep," Chris said. "Let's hit some golf balls into the Badlands."

Chris pulled the Jeep to the edge of a cliff and exited. The boys had not seen a single person during their exploration of the barren land, so they placed a golf ball on a tee and stuck it into the clay along the cliff.

Chris swung and made solid contact with the ball. It flew straight and high and hit the opposing cliff's edge, sending chunks of clay into the air. Ben lined up his shot and swung hard. His ball sailed forward and then faded left, knocking into a clay tower. The boys stood in awe of the view.

Ben and Chris turned around sharply. A car's engine approached, which caused their heart rates to elevate slightly. A state trooper's patrol car turned the corner and pulled in front of the Jeep. He exited his car and strolled toward them.

"You fellas enjoyin' the view?" the state trooper asked.

"Yes, sir," Ben said.

Ben's experience with police in his poor Portland neighborhood produced a brief negative attitude toward this authority figure.

Ben leaned against the golf club. He began to sweat

lightly with nerves. He knew that hitting golf balls into a National Park was frowned upon, but he was unaware of the actual legal ramifications of such an action.

"Did you drive here all the way from Massachusetts?" the state trooper asked, looking at the Jeep's license plates.

"Driving back to Boston from the West Coast," Chris said, consciously altering the Jeep's trajectory.

"Great," the state trooper said. "I just wanted to stop and make sure that you boys were alright. Enjoy the park."

"Thank you, officer," Ben said.

The state trooper strolled back toward his car and opened his door. Before he entered, he turned and looked at Chris.

"Did you fellas drive through Sturgis, by chance?" the officer asked.

"Yes, sir," Ben said.

He perspired profusely.

"Was it wild?" the officer asked. "I know that big motorcycle rally is happening this week."

Chris looked at Ben. Chris' hands began to shake.

"It looked like a lot of bikes showed up, but we just drove straight through," Ben said.

"I'll bet it was packed," the officer said. "Well, you boys have a safe journey."

"Thank you," the boys said in unison.

The state trooper waved, sat in his car, and drove away. Ben and Chris jumped into the Jeep and continued their cruise.

The otherworldly landscape shifted from brown clay, to purple, to yellow, to red rock formations. Ben's finger never left his camera trigger; he shot every new features that appeared.

Then, as if they never witnessed anything out of the ordinary, the landscape vanished and the boys found themselves in a flat grassland, void of physical features and full of roaming rams.

They passed the *Now Leaving Badlands National Park* road sign and reconnected with Interstate 90.

As the boys drove through South Dakota prairie land, the wind blew the Jeep's ragtop. The lack of scenery dulled the boys' minds. The sun set, but the Jeep had four hours of travelling until it reached Minneapolis.

After driving through prairies and farmland for the better part of the evening, the Jeep reached the wealthy Minneapolis suburban town and pulled into a driveway. Ben and Chris' pristine college friend, Geoffrey, opened the front door to greet them. Even at this hour of the night, Geoffrey exuded high-class style and demeanor.

Geoffrey's parents were asleep, so the boys went to the basement, where Geoffrey showed his guests to their sleeping quarters.

"Well, guys," Geoffrey said, "I'm glad you made it here safely and that you've decided to take a day off from driving tomorrow."

He smiled. His body language suggested that he was preparing to climb the stairs of his mansion and fall asleep in his plush bed.

"I know we didn't get a chance to catch up tonight since it was so late when you arrived, but I'll hear about your journey tomorrow. Rest up. I have a big day planned for us. Get ready to explore the Twin Cities."

"Thanks for letting us stay at your parents' house for two

nights," Ben said. "We couldn't pass through Minnesota in the summer without seeing you, buddy."

"I'm glad you made it," Geoffrey said.

Chris nestled into the couch in front of the massive television screen and Ben unrolled his sleeping bag on the floor near the billiards table.

"Well, boys, it's late," Geoffrey said. "I'll see you tomorrow. You'll never guess what I have planned."

Geoffrey strolled upstairs as Ben and Chris fell asleep, instantly.

# CHAPTER 9

Geoffrey stomped down the stairs, nearly tripping in his excitement. He leapt over Ben, who jolted awake in his sleeping bag. Geoffrey dashed to the basement window and pulled open the shade, which allowed Minnesota morning sunlight to flood the room.

Ben and Chris struggled to stay asleep; Ben buried his face into his sleeping bag, while Chris stashed his head between the couch cushions.

Geoffrey had been awake for over an hour. His auburn hair was combed perfectly, his thin-rimmed glasses perched on his long nose, and his red polo shirt was tucked into his khaki shorts. Though small in stature, Geoffrey projected summer affluence.

"Gentlemen, the day is upon us," Geoffrey said. "We have a shower down here and a shower on the main floor. We even have a steam shower on the second level, so take your pick."

Ben crawled from the depths of his sleeping bag cave

and began his morning exercises. Chris stumbled lazily to the basement shower. Geoffrey sat on the couch and turned on the television to ESPN's *SportsCenter*, where a baseball analyst was predicting the day's game between the Minnesota Twins and the Chicago White Sox.

After Ben completed his exercise routine, he decided to use the upstairs steam shower. He grabbed his clothes and climbed the basement stairs.

He entered the dining room and passed dark-wood hutches filled with gold-rimmed plates, sterling silverware, and a full-scale family portrait.

He exited the room and came into the mansion's entryway. Ben climbed the grand staircase and held onto the polished, oaken railing. He gazed upward at the crystal chandelier. When he reached the upstairs bathroom, he found the steam shower and eventually configured the technologically advanced system.

Ben returned downstairs and sat with Geoffrey and watched *SportsCenter*. When Ben and Chris appeared ready for the day, Geoffrey led them upstairs to the kitchen, where his family's butler had prepared a lavish breakfast of thin waffles, pineapple, mango, cinnamon oatmeal, and espresso-style coffee. The butler spread the meal on the kitchen island's dark, granite countertop. Ben's eyes widened at the healthy-yet-gluttonous display.

"Now this is a breakfast," Chris said. "I'm done with that hotel continental breakfast garbage."

"I've never had a gourmet breakfast like this," Ben said.

"Gourmet? This is one of our most basic meals," Geoffrey said. "We usually have quiche."

Ben gobbled every piece of food on his plate, while Chris

and Geoffrey pushed items to the side of their dishes because their palates were refined. Ben stood to clean his plate and thank the butler, but Geoffrey left his plate for the butler to gather. Chris followed Geoffrey's example.

Geoffrey led the boys through the mansion, through the front door, and into his silver sports car.

"Where are your parents today?" Ben asked. "I wanted to thank them for breakfast."

"They're at the country club today, of course," Geoffrey said. "My dad is playing golf with his business associates and my mom is having lunch with her social club."

Geoffrey turned on the radio, which projected smooth jazz through the car's cockpit. The car clung to the road as it accelerated around the tight neighborhood street corners. Expensive sports cars sat unused in adjoining driveways.

Ben gawked at the mansions. Massive, red-brick structures emerged through the old-growth trees. Most had doors with ornate door knockers. Some properties featured basketball and tennis courts, personalized to the owners. Front-porch columns projected socio-economic dominance in empirical Roman tradition. Iron gates protected these symbols of luxury from the common people of the outside world.

"There's a mansion on every corner," Ben said.

"Oh, these houses?" Geoffrey said casually. "These are my neighbors. See this house on the corner? The one with the three-story deck? That guy owns the Chicken Wing Spot franchise. And the house across the street? That guy is the C.E.O. of Ford."

"You have some high-rollers in your neighborhood," Chris said.

"Yeah, but my parents are nothing compared to these people," Geoffrey said.

"I don't know, man. Your house is pretty spectacular," Ben said.

"We don't have a tennis court, so I guess that makes our house more of a humble abode," Geoffrey said.

Ben snickered to himself. He thought about the house in which he was raised; a true humble abode. Ben had his own bedroom, which made him feel richer than most people in his neighborhood. His house had one bathroom and a small kitchen, which also served as the dining room. The small, boxed television had seven channels.

In order to save money, his parents would light a small fire in the fireplace during the winter instead of paying for the heating bill. Ben's childhood basement was full of mice and spiders.

Contrarily, Geoffrey came from a long lineage of wealth. His great-grandfather started a brewing company near Minneapolis in 1887. With the money he earned from his start-up business, he purchased stock in Standard Oil, John Rockefeller's monopoly. This continued stock purchasing strategy allowed him to accrue mass amounts of wealth.

Geoffrey's grandfather inherited a high standard of living, which allowed him to attend the University of Minnesota and obtain a job as an accountant at a firm that he eventually purchased with his family's fortune. Geoffrey's father was born into the wealthy Minneapolis family and was able to attend Columbia University through his father's connections.

Geoffrey's father inherited the family accounting firm and additional assets that contributed to the family dynasty's wealth and social status. Consequently, Geoffrey was born into one of the most established financial families in Minnesota.

"Where are we going, Geoff?" Chris asked.

"I want to show you the Mall of America," Geoffrey said. "Then, we'll eat lunch by my favorite lake. Then, I'm taking you to the Twins game. My family has club-level seats on the third base line."

"Thanks, Geoff!" Ben shouted. "I've never been to a professional baseball game before."

"And I've always wanted to see the Mall of America," Chris said.

"It's the biggest mall in the world, after all," Geoffrey said. "It even has its own amusement park inside."

"With roller coasters and everything?" Ben asked.

"Yes, sir," Geoffrey said. "And a log ride. That's my favorite."

The silver sports car strutted down the freeway, dodging between slower cars as it focused on its destination. An old sedan blocked the sports car's path, so it moved into another lane, knowing that the silver sports car was superior.

Geoffrey pulled his parents' car into a parking space and the boys strolled into the Mall of America; Geoffrey walked with arrogance, while Ben and Chris followed with humility. The entrance to the mall was massive; no shopping center in the world compared to its capacity for consumerism. Ben walked to a map of the mall.

"This mall has four Oakley sunglass stores?" Ben asked.

"And two Panda Express restaurants," Geoffrey added.

"A mall only needs one store where people can buy

sunglasses," Chris said. "Any more than that asks for bad economics."

"You're assuming that people come to this mall to *shop*," Geoffrey said.

"Why else would you go to a mall?" Ben asked.

"For the total American consumer experience, of course," Geoffrey said. "All of these people buy stuff here just to say that they bought it at the Mall of America."

Ben and Chris looked panoramically at the never-ending maze of stores and entertainment sources. Obese families funneled into stores with cartons of hot dogs, sodas, and cinnamon rolls.

Overweight mothers pushed strollers that contained fat children and dozens of shopping bags, while more obese fathers dug into their wallets in order to maximize their spending capacities. Most would end up spending more money than they possessed, forcing these families to purchase materialistic items through credit, which they could never afford to pay off.

"It's beautiful, isn't it?" Geoffrey asked. "This place brings in so much money and it has become the epicenter of American consumer culture. I love it!"

The three friends weaved between crowded lines. Human traffic flowed, but slowed at prime bottleneck areas, like intersections and food sample lines. All traffic lanes converged at the Mall's central vortex: the amusement park.

Ben looked up at the swirling roller coaster. Chris gazed at the log ride's steep descent into a deep pool. Geoffrey smirked at his friends awestruck expressions.

"Let's jump in line for the log ride," Geoffrey said. "All the other rides are weak."

After twenty minutes of wait time, the boys neared the log ride loading dock. In front of them, a drastically overweight man struggled to fit into his log seat. His equally glutinous wife inched her body into the log sleigh.

"These people need to lay off the soda and cake," Geoffrey said.

"They're probably really uneducated and poor," Chris said. "That's why they don't make conscious efforts to eat healthy. Plus, fatty foods are cheaper."

"They probably don't have a butler who makes their breakfast with egg whites every morning," Ben said.

Chris laughed; Geoffrey was too focused on elevating himself above the obese couple's misfortune to notice the verbal shot at his family's distance from the common American's socioeconomic situation. The couple fit into the log ride and created a massive splash at the end of the ride's first drop.

Ben, Chris, and Geoffrey each entered their own log seat. The logs departed the loading dock and floated in lukewarm water to a conveyor belt, which brought them to the top of a cliff.

The logs unhitched from the belt and floated weightlessly to the edge. The logs' momentum carried them over the edge of the cliff. Chris shrieked. Ben held his breath as he prepared for the pool's impact. A wave plunged over all three boys and soaked their entire wardrobes.

Geoffrey exited his log chariot first and shook the water from his hair. Ben and Chris walked damply to meet him near the center of the Mall and eventually made their way to the exit. The midday sun warmed the boys as they trekked through the enormous parking lot and their clothes were dry by the time the silver sports car appeared.

The warm wind circulated through the car as it drove closer to downtown Minneapolis. Geoffrey parked the car near a lake and led the group to taco stand. Ben ordered the cheapest street tacos he could find on the menu, but Geoffrey treated the boys to a round of Minnesota beers and an extravagant appetizer.

Sail boats floated on the lake near the hazy horizon, while paddle boarders worked closer to the shore. Dogs chased Frisbees and tennis balls on the grass. Ben drank his beer and looked across the lake at massive lakeside mansions. *The Great Gatsby* came to mind.

After their tacos and beers were gone, Geoffrey led the group on foot down a main road that took the boys to Target Field, where the Minnesota Twins would play the Chicago White Sox in a few hours.

A light crowd swirled around the stadium's entryway. The boys moved through it and entered an Irish pub across the street.

They sat on the deck and Geoffrey ordered another round of beers from a blonde waitress with a thick Minnesotan accent. She returned with three pints of amber ale. Geoffrey thanked her and she reentered the bar.

"Remind me how you got tickets to this game again," Ben said to Geoffrey.

"My parents have season tickets," Geoffrey said.

"That's cool," Chris said.

"I guess," Geoffrey said.

He shrugged his shoulders, implying nonchalance.

"We've always had these tickets," Geoffrey said. "My parents don't even use them and I'm at the point where I think these games are boring. Unless I bring friends, of course."

"How can these game get boring?" Ben asked.

"These seats are on the third base line in the club level, but I've gone to so many games that the experience has become so average," Geoffrey said.

"Why don't your parents come to the games?" Ben asked.

"They have season tickets to everything," Geoffrey said.

"Football, basketball, opera, you name it. They have so much money and they don't know what to do with it."

"That must be nice," Chris said. "That's my goal in life."

"Why, man?" Geoffrey said. "My parents aren't happy."

"How can someone be rich and unhappy?" Chris said.

"They have too much money and it consumes them," Geoffrey said. "They never even see their own kids. They rarely even spend time with each other. All my dad does is smoke cigars at the country club with business owners and politicians and talk about their stock portfolios. My mom lays by the pool all day and drinks Bloody Marys."

Geoffrey looked at the baseball stadium and took a drink of his amber ale. His eyes faced the stadium, but he was looking through it. To a distant memory.

"My parents don't work. They don't play," Geoffrey continued, as if speaking softly to the stadium. "They don't really contribute to the world in any way. They just collect expensive wine bottles that they don't even drink. My parents just bathe in their financial accounts and soak in complacency."

Geoffrey continued his gaze into his life's analysis. He looked through the stadium and into morals, ethics, and values. He continued to speak, but not to Ben or Chris; he spoke to his own conscience.

"My parents didn't even work to get rich," Geoffrey said.

"They were born into the upper class. I was born into the rich circle of America. I'll never have to work in my life. I have a *trust* fund, for God's sake. What has my family done to make the world a better place? Smoke its cigars, collect its sun rays, and hoard its wine? Money. *Ha!*"

Ben and Chris exchanged glances. Geoffrey divulged his soul with alcohol-induced fluidity. Ben embraced the unhappy confession of the monetarily rich; Chris yearned for the soul-bearing self-criticism of the upper class to end. Chris' dreams deflated with every word that Geoffrey spoke against the pursuit of riches.

"Your parents have a huge house and an awesome car," Chris said.

Geoffrey snapped his attention back to the table. His moment of vulnerability was over and he raised his guard again.

"Yeah, I wish they would buy a new one," Geoffrey said. "This silver sportster is slowing down."

Geoffrey and Chris laughed; Ben felt pity for Geoffrey's necessity to project affluence, stifling his true sentiments of unhappiness.

Ben pitied Chris' ultimate desire to gain wealth using Geoffrey's parents as an example.

Chris grew annoyed at Ben's lack of financial ambition, while Geoffrey envied Ben's cultivation of personal happiness over material wealth.

The waitress returned to the table. In an attempt to regain his image as a confident member of the affluent class,

Geoffrey ordered another round of drinks for his visitors. He winked at the waitress, who responded with a shy smile and blushed cheeks.

Chris steered the conversation to baseball statistics. He questioned Geoffrey about the financial prowess that he needed to achieve in order to afford season tickets to a professional baseball team; however, Ben wanted to discover the motivation behind Geoffrey's sudden exposure of wealth insecurity.

"Why don't your parents ever come to Twins games?" Ben asked. "I know we're not in the stadium yet, but this pre-game atmosphere is fun."

"I don't know," Geoffrey said. "I ask my dad to come with me every time I come, but he never wants to join me. He always has a meeting or an event to attend, which usually results in him drinking too much Scotch with his buddies."

"Why do your parents continue to buy season tickets if they never use them?" Ben asked.

"It's a status symbol in Minnesota, I suppose," Geoffrey said.

"I still don't understand how someone with high-class status can be unhappy," Chris said.

"I can," Geoffrey said. "My parents haven't worked toward anything in their entire lives. I'm unhappy because I've never had to work for anything in my life either. I knew I could get to college with my parents' money and connections. I never had an allowance as a kid, so I never had to budget in order to afford something I wanted. My parents just bought the thing for me. I've never learned how to make a meal for myself. My butler has always done it for me."

"Sounds like the life for me," Chris said.

"Honestly, not for me," Geoffrey said. "I've never had to pursue anything in my life. I would be much happier if I had to work hard and ride out a tough situation. Every event in my life has been so secure. I want some uncertainty. I want to pursue something."

"Like what?" Ben asked.

"I don't know, Benny," Geoffrey said. "I look at you. You're pursuing uncertainty in New York City. You're driving across the country toward an uncertain future and you're enjoying every minute of the adventure. You're pursuing the uncertainties of life through adventure and it's making you happy. You seem so fulfilled. I want something like that."

Geoffrey paused and sipped his beer. Neither Ben nor Chris dared interrupt him.

"But I'll settle for financial security and an unfulfilling existence, I guess," Geoffrey said.

"No way, Geoff," Chris said. "You have the life I want."

"Let's trade places then!" Geoffrey shouted with a cheery smile and shift in tone.

Geoffrey's projected affluence had returned again. He gave his Twins cap to Chris, who gave an impression of Geoffrey. The whole group laughed lightheartedly, but Ben lingered on Geoffrey's insight into the actual happiness levels up the upper echelon of American society.

Geoffrey paid for the drinks and tipped the waitress well. He thought about leaving his phone number on the receipt, but decided against the move and settled for a departing smile.

Feeling loose and slightly drunk, the boys left the Irish

pub and crossed the street to Target Field. They passed a bronzed statue of a former Twins star, which only Geoffrey recognized. A balding attendant with a yellow shirt scanned their tickets and the boys climbed the stairs to the club level.

Another attendant held the door for the three gentlemen and they entered the open-aired box. Geoffrey led them to the front row of the second level, which provided an upper-class view within close proximity to the field.

Sitting on the third base line, Ben looked across the field and saw the Minneapolis skyline shine in the setting sun.

A yellow-shirted attendant came to the front row of the club level and knelt next to Chris.

"Would you gentlemen care for a beer?" the attendant asked. "Perhaps some peanuts or nachos to get you started?"

"We'll take three beers and three nachos, please," Geoffrey said.

"I don't know if I can afford all that," Ben admitted.

"Don't worry. It comes with the price of season tickets," Geoffrey said. "We won't have to pay for a thing. Food and drinks are free and unlimited up here in the club level."

Ben's eyes widened at the thought of free food and drinks. He thanked Geoffrey for his hospitality, but felt sorry for Geoffrey's inherent need to project his social status, even in the company of friends.

After the *National Anthem* was performed, the first pitch flew across home plate. The Minnesota Twins took an early lead, but the White Sox regained control in the seventh inning. By the ninth inning, the White Sox had a two run lead. Most Twins fans began to leave the stadium.

The moon hung low in the sky and a cool breeze blew

through Target Field. The Twins' fourth slot batter stepped to the plate with two runners on base.

He swung hard at the first pitch and missed. Ben checked the replay on the stadium's big screen and saw the bat miss the ball by an inch. The next pitch crossed the plate at head level.

"*Strike!*" the umpire shouted.

The Twins' batter protested, but received no attention from the umpire. The batter returned to the plate and watched the White Sox's pitcher progress through his wind up. The ball flew toward home plate and the batter swung hard and made solid contact and the ball flew above the field.

A White Sox outfielder sprinted toward the back wall while tracking the ball with his turned head. The outfielder stepped onto the warning track and stopped. The ball sailed over the home run fence and the crowd erupted with excitement. The announcer shouted into the microphone.

"*Twins win! Twins win! 8 to 7!*"

The entire Twins dugout sprinted toward home plate to welcome their hero as he rounded third base. They shouted in celebration. The White Sox strolled off the field with a loss. Their heads hung in defeat, but they shook hands with the hosting team and acknowledged that the pursuit of victory was greater than this individual loss.

Ben, Chris, and Geoffrey left the club level and mingled with the evacuating crowd that swirled around the stadium in near pandemonium. The whole stadium's crowd projected their night's happiness on the nine players on the baseball field. Their projections returned the investment.

# CHAPTER 10

B en awoke in his sleeping bag. Chris snored on the couch. Geoffrey had fallen asleep in the reclining chair in the basement as the boys watched a replay of the Twins game. The television stayed on all night, so Ben watched a few minutes of *SportsCenter* before he moved. The sun began to poke through the half-open blinds, so Ben stood and opened them. Geoffrey startled awake and scanned the room. He was expecting to be in his bed, so he took a minute to adjust to his surroundings.

"Good morning, sunshine," Ben said.

"What time is it?" Geoffrey asked.

"About seven in the morning," Ben said.

"I slept down here all night, eh?" Geoffrey said.

"Thanks for taking us to the game last night, Geoff," Ben said.

"Any time," Geoffrey said.

Chris rustled in the couch cushions. He wanted Ben and Geoffrey's conversation to be a dream. He did not want to move from his couch cocoon and drive to Illinois.

"I hear you, Chris," Ben said. "How'd you sleep?"

"Like a rock," Chris mumbled through the couch cushion.

"Perfect," Ben said. "Let's get ready to go, buddy. It's a long way to Illinois."

Ben exercised on the floor while Geoffrey watched *SportsCenter* from his reclining chair. Chris emerged from the couch slowly and showered. When the boys were ready to leave, they packed the Jeep and returned inside the mansion. Geoffrey's parents were gone, but their butler made sandwiches for Ben and Chris to eat on the road, along with omelets to eat before they departed.

"Thanks for letting us stay with you, Geoff," Ben said. "It was great to see you."

"Thanks for calling," Geoffrey said. "I don't receive many visitors from the West Coast out here in Minnesota."

"The Twins game was amazing, Geoff," Chris said. "Thanks for taking us. We really appreciate it."

"Come back again and we'll go to another game," Geoffrey said. "If you visit during football season in the fall, we can see a Vikings game."

Ben jumped into the Jeep's driver seat, while Chris nestled into the passenger chair and prepared to fall asleep again. The Jeep reversed and then lurched forward onto the neighborhood road. It passed the lavish mansions of business executives and patent owners. Ben shifted into third gear and the Jeep growled as it passed a driveway with three new sports cars. After reaching the freeway, the Jeep headed south on Interstate 35 until it forked onto Highway 218 toward Cedar Rapids, Iowa. Eventually, the Jeep would rest in Mt. Vernon, Illinois for the night.

From the driver seat, Ben snapped a photograph of the *Welcome to Iowa* sign. It was slightly unfocused, but the effect reminded Ben that he needed to keep his mind on driving rather than photography. Once in Iowa, Ben noticed open space and corn fields. Every five minutes, the Jeep passed an old farm house with a wind-blown barn. Most barns had adjoining silos. The morning sun began to heat the Jeep's cockpit. Ben imagined the intense heat in the corn fields and concluded that farmers wore wide-brimmed hats in order to block the sun.

Ben wanted to photograph these images of the American spirit, but he feared that another animal would run in front of him, so he tapped the brakes and the Jeep jolted slightly. Startled, Chris popped his head up from his nap and looked around to gather his bearings.

"Where are we?" Chris asked, sleepily.

"Somewhere in Iowa," Ben said.

Chris observed the scenery for a few minutes before he came to the same conclusion.

"How could anyone live out here?" Chris asked.

"What do you mean?" Ben asked.

"There's nothing but fields," Chris said. "There's nothing to do. I don't see a movie theatre, a bar, or even a grocery store. Life out here would be so *boring*."

"Maybe these people are happy with the simple life," Ben suggested.

"How can *these people* be happy?" Chris said. "They can't make much money. I mean, how can anyone get rich by selling corn and wheat? Without extra money, these people can't buy toys. No wide-screen television. No speed boats.

And definitely no sports cars on these dirt side roads."

"Why do you assume that these folks need toys to be happy?" Ben asked. "Actually, why does *anybody* need material things to be happy? I don't get it."

"Because, Ben," Chris said, "having material possessions shows people that you have the money to afford these material possessions. If people can see that you have the money, then people know you're the boss."

Ben looked at the uniformed rows of corn as they zipped by his window lens. He observed a wooden farmhouse with peeling red paint that had no other residence in sight. Ben smiled.

"Does the ability to showcase your social status make you happy, Chris?" Ben asked.

"Of course it does!" Chris shouted.

"No it doesn't!" Ben shouted in return.

"Then what is point of making money?" Chris said.

"Is there a point to making *too* much money?" Ben asked.

"To bring happiness, of course," Chris said.

"Plenty of people throughout history have found happiness without money," Ben said. "People have lived in destitute poverty and were regarded as guides to happiness. Gandhi was poor. Emerson was poor for a while. Actually, Saint Francis of Assisi began his life as a rich man and he decided that he wasn't happy, so he gave all of his worldly possessions to the poor and he became a man who chose to live in poverty. He is regarded as one of the happiest people of all time."

"That's such a Catholic example," Chris said.

"I haven't considered myself Catholic for years, man," Ben said.

He felt his Saint Christopher medallion through his shirt and regretted his admission of denouncement toward the Church.

"How can someone live without a lot of money and still be happy, Ben?" Chris asked. "Explain this to me."

"I don't know," Ben said.

Ben looked out of his side window and watched another weathered barn pass through his lens. He pondered Chris' question before articulating his feelings toward happiness and money.

"All I know," Ben started, "is that I don't have any money to my name, yet I'm still happy. I don't even have a job or a solid vision of my future goals that will lead me toward money. But I'm happy right now. This adventure brings me pure joy. Since we left Oregon, I've cultivated a new sense of enjoyment for life. This adventure has brought me a sense of wonder for the world and the people in it and I want to foster that thrill for life. I don't need money to do that."

Chris shook his head and laughed. He acknowledged the variance between his own philosophies and those of his counterpart.

"I don't know how you can be happy without the slightest prospect of a job," Chris said. "If I wasn't on my way to work on Wall Street, I'd be miserable."

"You can't let your job define you," Ben said. "You can't let your social status determine your worth."

"That's all anyone has, Ben. A job and a social status," Chris said. "Those are the only attributes that the outside world sees. Those are the only qualities that define a person in the history books."

Ben stared through the windshield at the hot road that ran straight and disappeared into the horizon. He smoldered. He thought that all of the world's problems stemmed from attitudes like the one that Chris expressed. Ben knew that an all-world attitude shift would create a more peaceful culture, but greed and pride stood in the way. He felt helpless. If he couldn't change his friend's mind, how could he consider himself as a catalyst for change?

The boys drove for an hour in silence; each passenger contemplated the root of happiness. Chris wrestled with Ben's definition of money's place in a happy life because, though he never admitted this to his friend, Ben's words impacted his thinking.

Chris grabbed the camera and took a picture of the *Welcome to Missouri* road sign. He looked out the window and watched the Mississippi River approach from the left. Eventually, the highway aligned itself with the curvature of the surging river. The Jeep drove along the lifeline of the United States of America. Soon, a sign for the town of Hannibal appeared on the right side of the road. Chris noticed a caricature of Mark Twain on the sign. A question churned in his mind, but he needed Ben's help to answer it, so he decided to end the silence.

"Was Mark Twain from Hannibal, Missouri?" Chris asked.

"He grew up here," Ben said. "He used to watch boats move up and down the Mississippi River. That's where he got his pen name. *Mark Twain* was a riverboat call."

"How do you know this stuff?" Chris asked.

"I read it somewhere," Ben said.

"I read *The Adventures of Tom Sawyer* and *Adventures of*

*Huckleberry Finn* when I was in middle school," Chris said.

"Hannibal, this little town we're driving through, was the setting for both of those novels," Ben said.

"I thought Mark Twain was a pretty good writer," Chris said.

"He was brilliant," Ben said. "He once wrote, 'The perfection of wisdom, and the end of true philosophy is to proportion our wants to our possessions, our ambitions to our capacities, we will then be a happy and a virtuous people.' For all the critical acclaim and recognition he received for his writing, he lived a simple life."

"What does that mean?" Chris asked.

"Think about the characters that Mark Twain created: Tom Sawyer and Huck Finn," Ben said. "Both boys were dirt poor and lived in the backwoods of Missouri in a frontier town. Both boys were happy and pursued adventure. Mark Twain valued simplicity and experience over wealth and status."

"How do you know?" Chris asked.

"Because he wrote two of the greatest American novels in history about these themes and principles," Ben said.

Chris' eyes widened. He refocused his gaze to the passing town of Hannibal. He absorbed the images of the thick, swampy vegetation by the river. He noticed the comfortable intricacies of the small town homes and shops. He breathed in the deep humidity that the dense river provided. He tasted the dusty air.

The Jeep continued through Mark Twain's boyhood home town and headed for St. Louis. The environment shifted from a picturesque Twain novel to a big-city atmosphere.

Through the flat landscape, the Jeep's passengers saw the St. Louis skyline rise; a skyline they had only seen in social media photos. In the distance, the St. Louis Gateway Arch grew and became a prominent landmark. Though the Jeep drove to the East, it passed the Gateway to the West. Chris photographed the Arch with Ben's camera.

The Jeep crossed a bridge over the Mississippi River and Chris took a picture of the *Welcome to Illinois* road sign. The tired, sweaty vehicle continued for another hour until it stopped in a hotel parking lot in Mt. Vernon to rest for the night.

The humid ball of sun faded behind the Mississippi River, though the river had been out of viewing range for some time. Ben and Chris perspired as they carried their bags and trunks into the hotel. Chris' usually pristine hair now seemed ruffled by the humidity.

They took their bags to their room and decided to visit the hotel bar, per usual. They wanted to order a local beer, so they asked the bartender for his best recommendation.

Since the hotel resided so close to St. Louis, the bartender recommended Budweiser. Chris and Ben laughed at the thought of a local beer being the most popular domestic beer in the United States. Out of consistency, they each ordered a Budweiser.

"You know, Ben," Chris said, "I think you're crazy for coming with me to New York."

"What do you mean?" Ben asked.

"You don't have a prospect of finding a job out there," Chris said. "How are you going to survive? You shouldn't have come with me. That was a stupid decision."

"You're the one who asked me to make the journey with

you," Ben said.

"I know. I'm sorry for asking," Chris said. "I shouldn't have asked you to move to New York. You had a better potential for a future in Portland."

"Shut up, man," Ben said. "I'll be fine on the East Coast. Besides, I have no more prospects for a job in Portland than I do in New York."

"What if you end up working a dead-end job? You'll turn out like those corn farmers that we passed today," Chris said. "You'll be miserable. And it's all my fault for asking you to travel with me."

"Who cares if I don't make any money at my job, Chris?" Ben shouted. "I don't need to find happiness through my damn bank account and stock portfolio!"

The bartender, who despised unruly customers, turned and looked at Ben. He lifted an eyebrow, but returned to cleaning pint glasses at the wash station.

"Calm down, Ben," Chris said. "I'm just giving you a hard time."

"As long as a person feels like he's making a difference in the world, that person will feel happiness," Ben said. "I just want to make a positive change in the world we live in. I want to leave our world in better shape than it was when I got here."

"I'll make bundles of money and I'll make a difference in the world at JP Morgan Chase," Chris said.

"How will you make a difference in the world?" Ben asked.

"I'll help other people make more money," Chris said.

"How much money will you take from people in order to get them rich?" Ben asked.

"I don't know," Chris said. "I think my commission percentage is high, even for Wall Street."

"What if you take that commission percentage from people's funds that don't make them money?" Ben said. "Will that difference you're making still make you happy?"

"Well, Ben," Chris said, "as long as I'm making commission, I'll be happy. People who bet on the financial industry know what they're getting into. They know that there are risks involved with financial firms."

"I hope this does make you happy, Chris. I really do," Ben said.

"I've aimed for this goal my whole life," Chris said. "My job title will be my identity for the next thirty years."

"I'll change your philosophy someday," Ben said with a light-hearted smile.

"Benjamin Emerson," Chris said, "we've driven all the way from *Oregon* and you still haven't changed my philosophy. I still want to be the richest man in the world."

A grizzled man sat at the end of the bar. His attention focused on the televised baseball game that played above the liquor shelf, but his focus shifted to the Ben at the mention of his name. The man looked down at his beer, picked it up, and walked toward them. He walked with intent; his eyes glared with trained focus.

Ben saw the man approach. He wore a thick canvas jacket that nearly matched his worn baseball cap. The man's beard looked trimmed-yet-unkempt and the tattoo of a sniper rifle's crosshairs exuded from his right hand. His paint-stained jeans and thick military boots suggested a tough, weathered demeanor.

The man sat next to Ben, placed his beer on the bar, and

glared at Ben with intensity. Ben began to tremble slightly, so he grabbed his pint glass to calm his nerve.

"Your name is Benjamin Emerson?" the man asked.

"Yes, sir," Ben said with fabricated confidence.

"You're from Oregon?" the man asked.

"Yes I am," Ben said.

"What was your father's name?" the man asked.

"David Emerson," Ben said, reluctant to give his father's information to this intimidating character.

The man's focus narrowed.

"Did he die in Iraq?" the man asked.

"He did," Ben said, taken back by the question.

Chris looked at Ben with a confused expression; his body language asked Ben to explain the situation, but Ben felt lost in the context of the conversation. He flipped through every memory catalogue he could find, but he could not place the man's face, nor could he decipher the context of the situation. The man took his hat off and placed it on the bar next to his pint glass. His shaved head produced a further image of a tough exterior.

"I'm First Sergeant Paul Adams," the man said. "I served alongside your father in Iraq with the U.S. Marine Corps. I was with him on the day he died."

Ben stared at the man. A knot formed in his throat. Ben wanted to ask Paul so many questions and he tried to speak, but the knot in his throat suppressed the words. He began to cry. The man put a hand on his shoulder.

After Ben cried for a few minutes, he wiped his eyes and took a drink of his beer. He looked at Chris, and then return his focus to Paul Adams.

"Did you know my dad well?" Ben asked.

"I did two tours of duty in Iraq with him," Paul said. "He talked about you and your mother every single day. When I heard your friend say your name, I had no doubt that you were David's son. He also talked about Oregon and how much he loved it, so that clarified everything for me. I had to come over and introduce myself."

"Well it's great to meet you, Paul," Ben said. "You know, I didn't see my dad much when I was in high school because he fought in Iraq for so long. Can you tell me about him?"

Paul smiled as he recalled specific memories.

"Your dad was strong-willed," Paul said.

"How so?" Ben asked.

"He fought any injustice that he saw, whether that was for or against his commanding officers. I remember one time, about three weeks before he was killed, your dad and I were infiltrating a neighborhood near Baghdad with a group of six Marines. Our mission was to knock on doors and find information about suspected rebels. A middle-aged man answered the door and he brought us inside his home. The man's wife and son were sitting on the couch when we entered the living room. The man asked his wife to leave and she refused because her son was sleeping on the couch. The man wound his arm back and slapped his wife in the face. She left the room crying, of course. Your dad sat the man on the couch and scolded him in fluent Arabic for 30 minutes. Finally, the man brought his wife into the living room and apologized profusely. Your dad continued to scold the man in Arabic until he cried in front of his wife! It was great!"

Ben laughed and so did Paul.

"That's something you would do, Benny," Chris said. "I

didn't know your dad spoke Arabic."

"Neither did I," Ben said.

"Your dad was wicked smart," Paul said. "He spoke Arabic, Farsi, and Spanish. He knew so much about Iraqi culture that he embarrassed our commanding officers in briefing meetings on a weekly basis."

Ben laughed again.

"It's terrible that he died by friendly fire," Ben said.

"Friendly fire?" Paul said. "Is that what they told you?"

"Yeah," Ben said. "A military officer came to our house when I was 16 and told my mom and I that he died by friendly fire in a small gun battle."

"That's bullshit," Paul said. "Our government would spin the story that way. I'll tell what really happened. I held him as he died."

Ben looked at Chris with amazement. He returned his attention to Paul with a focus that would not fade.

"Your father and I were part of a team that was supposed to infiltrate another neighborhood near Baghdad and find a specific man who had ties to al-Qaeda," Paul said. "We knocked down the door of his apartment and handcuffed our suspect. We sat him down for questioning. Your dad spoke to him in Arabic and the man provided no information about al-Qaeda or any other rebel activity. As we found out later, this man had no ties to any rebel or terrorist group; he was just a normal dad trying to live in a war-torn country."

Chris leaned into the conversation; his interest intensified.

"Jackson, a notoriously hotheaded member of our six-man team, got frustrated and he shot the man in the head because we were getting no information. Your dad went ballistic and tried to subdue our teammate, and for good reason. Your dad was quite the moral crusader, so he wanted Jackson tried for war crimes."

The bartender heard this conversation occurring, so he refilled all three pint glasses without the men noticing. The refills were not added to the bill.

"When our buddy shot that Iraqi father, other Iraqis from the apartment complex rushed out of their doors and looked in the room," Paul said.

Ben's eyes began to fill with tears, but he remained focused on the storyteller.

"Dozens of people stood by the door with guns and the situation was intensifying quickly. I was nervous as hell. I thought the Iraqi mob would execute us on the spot, and rightfully so. Your dad stepped to the front of the mob and spoke in Arabic."

"I didn't know he was that good at Arabic," Ben whispered.

"He explained the situation with complete honesty and apologized on behalf of the United States for the unfair treatment of the Iraqi people. The mob began to defuse, but Jackson pushed your father and rebuked him for talking to the Iraqis, so the situation intensified. Jackson pointed his gun at the mob, so the mob returned the action."

Ben felt his heart quicken pace. His breathing shortened.

"Your father spread his arms across the doorway and put his entire body between the gun-toting mob and our whole unit. Jackson shouted and the mob fired and they shot your father multiple times in the chest. After they shot him, they dispersed. I dragged your father into the room and locked the apartment door. He gave me something from his vest pouch and he died in my arms."

Ben continued to look at Paul with amazement, admiration, and sadness.

"When our military police unit arrived," Paul said, "Jackson said that our detained Iraqi father was shot during a firefight and that one of us fired back and accidentally killed David. That's the story the government ran with in order to cover up the war crime that we all knew had happened. I spoke out against Jackson, but my C.O. silenced me. So, when my contract was done, I left the Marines. Your dad showed me the right path to justice."

Ben felt another knot in his throat and he cried softly and coherently.

"Ben," Paul said, "your father was a hero. So many soldiers claim that they're fighting for their country, when all they want to do is kill people based on hate and cultural bias. But your father, he wanted to change the world. As paradoxical as this sounds, your father was a peaceful soldier."

Paul placed his hand on Ben's shoulder.

"I have something for you," Paul said. "I live about three blocks away from here. Come with me, fellas."

Paul paid for the beers and the boys walked down the streets of Mt. Vernon until they reached Paul's single-story house. They entered the living room and Ben noticed a framed picture of Paul with his crew of Marines; David Emerson's kind smile warmed the picture of the warriors.

Ben and Chris sat on the couch while Paul went into his room. He came back a few minutes later with a tattered journal and gold chain with a medallion. He gave them both to Ben.

"Your father wrote in his journal every day," Paul said. "It was on his bed the day he died, so I picked it up and kept it. I didn't want your mother to see it because he wrote with gruesome detail, but I think you're old enough to know what your father saw and how he perceived the war."

Ben opened it and flipped through the pages. His father's handwriting felt like his father's voice.

"And he wore this medallion of Saint Francis of Assisi every day," Paul said, pointing to the gold chain. "He said that it reminded him to remain peaceful, even in times of war."

Ben gripped the medallion. It was tattered, just like the journal, but he felt an aura of serenity from its presence.

"Your father hated the so-called *War on Terror*," Paul said. "He knew that our military was in the Middle East to gain control of major oil-producing countries. Also, he thought that President Bush wanted to finish off his father's war with Saddam. Your dad's mission was to promote a peaceful image of the United States to every Iraqi that he met. David wanted to learn and absorb their culture so that he could eventually bring peace to the Middle East through diplomacy and service instead of with violence and force. He thought our military presence in the Middle East was no better than the presence of Saddam's regime or al-Qaeda's reign of terror."

Ben held his father's journal tightly. Paul looked at the picture of his former Marine crew. His eyes stared into memory.

"David wanted this concept of American greed and hunger for power to end," Paul said. "He wanted everyone

131

to promote wisdom and love. What a novel concept."

o    o    o

When Ben and Chris returned to their hotel, they each sat on their beds. Chris fell asleep instantly. Ben tried to sleep, but he only thought about his father. Ben removed his Saint Christopher medallion from his own gold chain and placed it on his father's old chain so it hung next to Saint Francis of Assisi. Ben placed his empty chain in his backpack and he hung his father's chain around his neck. Saint Francis of Assisi and Saint Christopher now hung close to his heart; now Ben travelled with a sense of peace and humility.

# CHAPTER 11

Ben awoke before the sun rose. He tried to return to his sleeping state, but his mind focused only on the previous night's conversation. He thought about his father and wrestled with the new pictures of his father's last days. Ben's alarm would sound in over an hour, so he rolled over and turned it off.

Ben grabbed his personal journal, his father's journal, and a pen and walked to the hotel exercise area. He completed his customary push-ups, sit-ups, and pull-ups with hopes that this would clear his mind. Exercise helped, but he needed another outlet, so went to the lobby.

The concierge sat behind the counter; his computer occupied his interest. Ben filled a paper cup with decent coffee and sat in a leather chair by a coffee table that was littered with magazines. He opened his journal and wrote about yesterday's encounter with First Sergeant Paul Adams. When he finished his own thoughts, he picked up his father's journal. When Ben read his father's handwriting, he heard his father's calm voice.

*June 5, 2005*

*I saw an Iraqi child die today. He walked by a car bomb when it exploded; the car bomb was meant for the gunner vehicle in my platoon. I jumped out of our Humvee and grabbed the kid. He died in my arms.*

*I don't understand how people can be so cruel to each other. Why do people feel that killing other people will solve their social issues? I understand that poverty drives people to do desperate things. That's why I joined the military originally; I was dirt poor. I understand that the U.S. military has invaded their homeland and that's why some Iraqis want us dead. I'd be pissed if someone invaded us, so I can empathize with their feelings. Our commanding officers need to be more aware of that fact. It's ironic that our military claims to fight for our freedom when, in reality, we're suppressing the freedom of Iraqi and Afghan people by occupying their land with guns and troops.*

*We need to fight a war with peace instead of guns (says the guy holding a gun in one hand and a pen in the other).*

*David E.*

Ben read through a few more entries from his father's journal. Reading his father's perspective on his personal war experiences gave Ben an opportunity to listen to his father; it allowed Ben to progress toward closure.

The hotel's grandfather clock chimed after an hour, so Ben returned to his room. Chris was sleeping, so Ben showered and packed the car. When Chris awoke, he thanked Ben for his productive morning and he offered to drive the first shift; this offer came from empathetic motivations. The day's journey would take the Jeep through Indiana, Kentucky, and West Virginia, where it would rest at the estate of Chris' uncle.

*CD Number One* played quietly through the stereo as the Jeep neared Indiana. Ben remained silent for a half hour; his mind focused on the new details of his father's life. He needed time to process. He wished he could talk to his dad, or his mom, for that matter. He wondered if she knew the truth about his father's death.

Ben held his camera and focused his lens on the *Welcome to Indiana* road sign and clicked the camera's trigger. He snapped four photographs, flipped through his work on the camera's digital screen, and kept the highest quality picture. Soon, the Jeep entered the Hoosier National Forest. Instinctively, Ben photographed the forest road sign.

"That's a fitting name for a forest in Indiana," Chris said.

"I wonder if Gene Hackman has visited," Ben said.

"*Hoosiers* was a great movie," Chris said. "Gene Hackman was the reason I wanted to play basketball in middle school. I was always too short, though."

The Jeep sped through the cloudy, forested landscape of lower Indiana. Sooner than Ben expected, the *Welcome to Kentucky* road sign appeared as the Jeep crossed the Ohio River, so he photographed the sign and the water feature.

"We're driving through Louisville?" Ben asked. "I didn't know we were going to drive through Louisville. I always played as Louisville on college football video games."

"You mean *Loo-a-vull?*" Chris asked with an exaggerated

southern accent.

"*Lew-ee-vill,*" Ben said.

"No, you have to say it like your mouth is full of cotton balls," Chris said. "*Loo-a-vull.*"

"I blame the French," Ben said.

"Always blame the French," Chris said.

The Jeep cruised on Interstate 64 through Kentucky. The sun emerged from the clouds and the humidity and heat rose within the ragtop cockpit. Low-hanging trees and wide-brimmed grass covered the landscape. Occasionally, Ben photographed elaborate horse ranches; elegant horses galloped along pristine grass fields encased in white fences that matched the barns and estate houses.

"Now these people know how to live," Chris said. "Those barns must cost a small fortune."

"How is this barn different that the barns we saw in Iowa?" Ben asked.

"Look at how well they're painted," Chris said. "And a horse isn't cheap to buy or maintain."

"The farms in Iowa had horses," Ben said.

"But look at how much land these horse ranches have," Chris said.

"No more land than the corn fields in Iowa," Ben said.

"But these Kentucky ranchers project a better image, so they must be living the dream," Chris said.

"You're judging a book by its cover, man," Ben said. "Maybe these people care more about their paint than they do about their family's happiness. Maybe the Iowa farmers love life and don't care about painting their barn."

"Well, the Kentucky Derby doesn't take place in Iowa, so Kentucky ranchers know how to live," Chris said.

"Well, the Iowa Caucus determines the presidential elections, so they sure are smart in Iowa," Ben said.

"Alright, fair enough," Chris said.

The Jeep approached the Daniel Boone National Forest. Ben gripped his camera and photographed the natural beauty of the untouched wilderness. The Jeep strolled through the tree-lined road without another traveler on the highway. Once through the forest, Chris noticed a road sign.

"Kentucky bourbon," Chris said.

"What about it?" Ben asked.

"We're in Kentucky. We should visit a Kentucky bourbon distillery," Chris said.

"That sounds expensive," Ben said.

"Not when Wall Street's paying for it," Chris said.

Chris pulled the Jeep off and onto the next exit. He followed the blue arrow that directed the Jeep to a bourbon distillery that was surrounded by the Daniel Boone National Forest. The Jeep pulled into a gravel parking lot. Ben and Chris exited and strolled toward the log cabin. As they entered the porch area, Chris saw a sign that read *Log Cabin Distillery: Real Kentucky Bourbon* and the boys walked underneath it and into the log cabin itself.

They saw no one in the entryway, so Ben approached the counter cautiously, as he felt unsure whether or not the distillery was open to visitors. A man in his mid-thirties approached the counter from the worker's side. His shirt label bore the insignia of the whiskey bottles that surrounded the back walls.

"Good afternoon, gentlemen," the distiller said, with a noticeable southern twang.

"How's it going?" Ben said.

"What brings you fellas to Log Cabin today?" the distiller asked.

"We want to drink some whiskey," Chris said.

"Well, you've come to the right place," the distiller said. "Would you guys like a tour of the distillery, or do you want to jump straight to tasting some bourbon?"

"I don't know if we have time for a tour, but we'd love to try your varieties of bourbon," Chris said.

The distiller led the boys to the back room bar. A single log served as the bar top table. The entire interior of the tasting room was covered in wood and the barstools were made of pure tree. The Log Cabin moniker suited the establishment perfectly.

Ben and Chris sat at the bar. Five minutes later, the distiller brought five more shot glasses full of whiskey and set them in front of Chris. He returned with five shot glasses, which he gave to Ben.

Each shot glass contained bourbon of a varying shade of brown, the distinct color of bourbon. The distiller described each bourbon with a refined vocabulary, which Ben expected to reflect in his taste buds, although he knew that he did not possess a refined palate.

Chris sipped his bourbon flight and commented on each whiskey using the same vocabulary that the distiller used when giving his explanation. Ben noticed that each bourbon varied in taste, but in short, he knew that each drink tasted like good bourbon.

"So, Ben," Chris said. "You haven't mentioned Samantha in a few days. Are you finally over that blood-sucking vampire?"

"Honestly, no," Ben said.

"What do you mean?" Chris asked. "I thought you were on a mission to find a free-spirited, experience-life, save-the-world kind of girl. Like that Lucy chick we met in South Dakota."

"I am," Ben said. "But if Samantha called me right now, I would get back together with her."

"You're an idiot for saying that," Chris said.

Ben sipped his bourbon and thought about his previous statement, which he immediately regretted making. He did not believe that he would take Samantha back, even if she asked. He began to understand that he needed someone who actually respected him. *Or, maybe I would take her back*, Ben thought.

His mind wandered from Samantha, to bourbon, to Lucy. Her feathery-blonde hair drifted down onto her cheeks. Her soft-yet-determined blue eyes seemed to hold the whole world's altruistic ambitions. Her light-yet-powerful voice provided a sense of purpose to each word she spoke.

"Lost in thought, are we, Benny?" Chris said.

Ben snapped form his daydream.

"Just promise me something," Chris said. "If Samantha calls, don't answer."

Chris shot the remainder of his bourbon and slammed the glass on the bar top. He tipped the distiller well for his hospitality and Ben thanked him for his service. After finishing their tastes, they left Log Cabin. Ben took his shift in the driver seat.

As the Jeep pulled onto the freeway, Ben saw the *Welcome to West Virginia* road sign, so he insisted that Chris take a photograph, which he did. Once in West Virginia, the landscape shifted from forest with vibes of civilization to dense hills with no indications of culture or life. Ben felt a strange sense of loneliness in the hills; the rising landscape blocked the sun and created eerie shadows on the road. The forest grew thick as darkness dawned in the late afternoon.

"Damn," Chris said. "These hills are blocking my cell phone reception. I'll bet we don't get service until we reach Uncle Joseph's house."

"How far is that?" Ben asked.

"About an hour," Chris said.

The Jeep drove over pothole after pothole on the West Virginia section of Interstate 64. Every billboard promoted coal mining, which told Ben that coal was a major industry in the hills.

Recently, the United States government had publicly announced its choice to move away from coal-powered energy due to its contamination of the air. President Barack Obama's administration vowed to increase alternative energy options, like solar and wind power; therefore, some billboards on Interstate 64 portrayed President Obama as an incarnation of the devil himself.

"I wonder what color West Virginia votes during election time," Ben said sarcastically.

"I'd say West Virginia votes red and as far to the right as possible," Chris said.

The boys laughed at their own obvious political banter. Ben increased the stereo volume and a familiar rap song about a drive-by shooting in South Central Los Angeles blasted through the ragtop cockpit. The Jeep stumbled over another pothole, followed by another, then another.

*Boom!*

The driver-side tire exploded and the Jeep swerved to the right. Ben over-corrected the steering wheel and the Jeep drifted left into oncoming traffic. An oncoming semi-truck honked as the Jeep swerved into its lane. Ben cranked the steering wheel the opposite direction and the semi-truck sped by the out-of-control Jeep.

The back end of the Jeep fishtailed, so Ben corrected again and evened out, but it still wanted to pull left. The Jeep wanted to drag left with all its power. Ben cranked the steering wheel to the right and held it with all of his strength, but the back tires jumped back and forth on the bumpy asphalt. Ben felt the air leave his lungs.

Ben slammed the brakes and drifted onto the highway's dirt shoulder, where the Jeep skidded to a stop.

Chris' face turned white and his hands shook with fear and adrenaline. Ben hyperventilated. His knuckles gripped the steering wheel and turned white with live rigor mortis. Neither boy moved for a perceived eternity.

"Shit, Benny!" Chris shouted, breaking the silence.

"What happened? What the hell was that?" Ben said.

"I think we blew a tire," Chris said.

Ben exited the Jeep and looked at the wheel well, which now contained a scrap of rubber tire. Chris unlatched the Jeep's spare tire, which hung on the trunk flap. He searched his glove box for a ratchet to unscrew the shredded tire's bolts, but he found nothing.

Ben grabbed a shirt from his backpack and unscrewed the bolts by hand, which took more force than anticipated. His adrenaline rush aided his bolt-loosening strength.

They lifted the Jeep up with the jack. Once the tire

shreds were discarded, Ben and Chris hoisted the new spare tire in place and hand-cranked the bolts to secure the tire.

"Without a ratchet, we can't secure these bolts enough to drive safely for another hour to your uncle's house," Ben said.

"You're right, man," Chris said. "What should we do?"

"We don't have cell phone service, so we can't call anyone," Ben said.

"We could wait for someone to drive by," Chris suggested.

"The only other traveler I've seen was the semi-truck that almost destroyed us," Ben said.

Ben and Chris looked around the forested area.

"I see a dirt road up ahead," Chris said. "Let's drive onto it and see if we can find some help. We'll have to drive slowly, but maybe we'll find somebody with a ratchet."

"That's our only option, I think," Ben said.

The boys jumped into the Jeep. Ben drove slowly on the highway shoulder until it reached the dirt road entrance, where he turned right. The rough road wound through dense forest and around a hill.

Though the Jeep moved slowly by necessity, the road seemed long. The sounds of Interstate 64 faded quickly. Chris looked through the trees and saw no signs of civilization. The Jeep wound around another hill and the road began to descend.

Soon, the Jeep approached a fork, so Ben decided to follow the path that featured tire tracks. The forest produced a dangerous silence.

The boys saw it at the same time: a group of four double-wide trailers that sat in the trees just off of the dirt road. Ben and Chris looked at each other with curious caution. Ben crept the Jeep to the edge of the trailers' territory and idled. Chris urged Ben to shut the Jeep off, but Ben remained still in case a getaway was needed.

As the Jeep idled, Ben felt an eerie silence emerge from the woods. Nothing moved or made a noise.

"We're in the backwoods of West Virginia, Ben," Chris said. "This is where those lawless hillbillies live. This is where people house their massive illegal drug operations. This is where people get lost and don't get found."

"Chill out, Chris," Ben whispered. "You hop in the driver seat. I'm going to knock on this trailer door. If a dangerous person answers, we'll get out of here quickly. If a friendly face answers, we'll borrow their tools, fix our tire, and continue on to Uncle Joseph's house in Princeton. Deal?"

"Deal," Chris said.

Ben opened the driver door and Chris slid into the driver seat. The Jeep's engine rumbled in preparation to escape the hills.

"Ben," Chris whispered. "Be careful. Keep your eyes open."

Ben walked cautiously toward the front door of a trailer. He wondered if his father felt this same sense of adrenaline and awareness when he was infiltrating homes in Iraq.

Ben felt the Saint Christopher and Saint Francis medallions on his heart. An overwhelming sense of calm focus overcame him. He continued to walk with cautious confidence toward the trailer's front door.

He climbed the three foldable stairs and opened the screen door, which groaned laboriously. Ben knocked on

Tom Malone

the front door and took four steps backwards. His hands shook from nerves and his left cheek twitched, which it often did when Ben's fight-or-flight instincts arose.

He remembered this feeling from high school sports games. He knew that his dad felt the same sensations during his tours in Iraq.

The trailer door creaked open. A heavy boot poked through the ajar door, followed by a shotgun barrel. A burly, middle-aged man stood firmly behind the loaded shotgun. His belly protruded through his overalls; the straps were covered by a thick, salt-and-pepper beard. The man stared at Ben.

"Who are ya and what d'ya want?" the burly man asked.

His gruff voice twanged with a distinct accent.

"We, we, we have flat tire," Ben stammered. "Do you have a ratchet that we can borrow?"

"Where you boys from?" Burly Man asked.

"I'm from Oregon," Ben said.

"Then what're ya doin' here?" Burly Man asked with a gruff tone.

"My friend and I are driving to his Uncle Joseph's house in Princeton," Ben said.

"Joseph who?" Burly Man asked.

"Joseph Morgan," Ben said.

"Joe Morgan owns half the state of West Virginia," Burly Man said.

Another trailer's front door opened and a skinny man with a trucker hat walked toward the Jeep. His expression suggested inquiry and suspicion.

"Hey, Billy Ray!" Burly Man shouted. "These folks are goin' to Joe Morgan's house!"

"Joe Morgan?" Billy Ray said. "He own half the state. Say, Ronnie, isn't it about time for us to pay off Joe Morgan again?"

"It sure is, Billy Ray," Burly Man said. "He always sends his runners to us around the Fourth of July. He's a good American, after all."

"We gotta do what we can to keep those state troopers off our backs," Billy Ray said.

Ben turned and looked at Chris in the Jeep. He noticed an expression of disappointment on Chris' face for a moment, followed by masked fear.

"What was it you boys needed from us again?" Ronnie asked Ben. "A ratchet for your tire?"

"Yes, sir," Ben said.

His voice trembled and his hands shook, so he put them in his pocket.

"Well, come on into my trailer and we'll find you a ratchet," Ronnie said.

Ronnie stomped into the trailer. The screen door slammed shut behind him. Ben followed hesitantly. He wanted to avoid the trailer, but he felt obligated to accept Ronnie's invitation.

His senses fired. He noticed Billy Ray's hand movement. He heard a bird flutter from one tree to another. He smelled firewood burning in the woods nearby, followed by a stink that exuded from the trailer.

Ben entered the trailer cautiously. The trailer's kitchen was clean, which surprised Ben based on Ronnie's burly demeanor. The screen door slammed behind Ben, which made him jump. Ronnie motioned for Ben to sit in a wooden kitchen chair, so Ben obliged.

"You want some coffee, son?" Ronnie asked Ben.

"No, thanks," Ben said.

Ronnie reached into a closet and searched for a ratchet. Ben watched carefully. He suspected that Ronnie was searching for something other than a ratchet. *How did I end up in this backwoods trailer?* Ben wondered. *Is this where my story ends?*

Ben heard rustling in the closet. Ronnie emerged with a ratchet and an envelope, which he placed in his jacket quickly.

Ronnie exited the trailer, so Ben followed. They returned to the Jeep, where Billy Ray was leaning against the open window. Billy Ray laughed earnestly, while Chris laughed uncomfortably.

Ronnie handed the ratchet to Ben, who knelt by the Jeep's spare tire and tightened the bolts. Ben stood and turned. Ronnie approached and stood uncomfortably close to Ben. Ronnie reached into his jacket pocket with a quick motion.

Ben's awareness peaked. Ronnie removed his hand from his jacket and shoved and envelope against Ben's chest.

"Give this to Uncle Joe," Ronnie said. "And make sure you tell him where it came from."

"We will," Ben said.

Ben's nerves rattled. He handed the ratchet to Ronnie and jumped into the Jeep's passenger seat.

"Get out of here, man," Ben said in a panicked whisper. "Hustle."

The Jeep spun and slid in the loose dirt. It sped toward the highway on the same bumpy dirt road. Ben and Chris were silent until the Jeep returned to the paved highway.

"That place was eerie," Chris aid.

"You're telling me," Ben said. "What line of business do you think those guys were in?"

"They must not be any good at their job if they live in trailers in the backwoods of West Virginia," Chris said.

Ben reached into his pocket and pulled out the envelope. It was unsealed, so Ben opened the flap. He reached inside the envelope and removed its contents: 2,500 dollars.

He showed the money to Chris, who glanced at the pile of cash and then at the windshield. He looked pensive.

"That doesn't surprise me," Chris said. "My Uncle Joe rose to West Virginia political power quickly. He's always been a smooth talker and he's always had money and power on his mind. I'm not surprised that he used bribery to reach the top of the political power rankings."

Chris breathed heavily, partly to calm his growing anger and partly to suppress his fear of the current situation. He was disappointed with his uncle's political tactics. Chris wanted to believe that Uncle Joe's intentions and political strategies possessed ethics and virtues. He wanted to believe that this 2,500-dollar bribe was just a blemish on his uncle's character, but based on Uncle Joe's demeanor, Chris had always known that his uncle was a corrupt politician. This 2,500-dollar bribe reinforced that idea.

The Jeep trotted along the pothole-ridden tollway. It moved slower than usual as it tried out its new tire. The unused treads enhanced the Jeep's turning confidence, but it still felt unsure about its ability to increase its speed.

Ben placed the 2,500-dollar stack in the envelope, sealed it, and tossed it in the glove compartment.

"Let's not mention that money to my uncle," Chris said.

"Why not?" Ben asked.

"If Uncle Joseph wants to be a political leader, I want him to gain power ethically," Chris said.

"What if he gets in trouble? What if Ronnie comes after him?" Ben asked.

"Uncle Joe knew what he was doing when he made an illegal deal," Chris said.

Ben raised his eyebrows and gazed through the windshield. He was astonished at Chris' disdain for Uncle Joseph's capacity to gain power and profit despite ethical tactics.

Chris was disappointed in his uncle's methods. He wanted to discuss his uncle's political ethics when the Jeep reached Princeton. He wanted to lecture Uncle Joe about the responsibility that comes with political acquisition; Uncle Joseph was running for the Governor's seat of West Virginia and Chris wanted to believe that his uncle was worthy of the position.

"What are we going to do with this money?" Ben asked.

"I don't know," Chris said, "but it won't line the pockets of a corrupt politician. Even if that corrupt politician is my uncle."

The Jeep exited the tollway and drove into Princeton. The town was quiet and empty as the sun set. Coal mines and processing factories lined the town's borders, while small shops and train tracks filled its interior. The road signs looked rusted and weather-beaten. Some road signs rested on the ungroomed wild grass along the road.

As the Jeep stopped at a red light, it felt an aura of blue-collared, industrial work ethic from the gritty homes and businesses.

The road led the Jeep out of downtown and into a forested hill. It turned onto Morgan Drive, a tree-lined dirt road that weaved through pristine fields. As the road neared its end, the trees thinned and unveiled a colonial mansion with three-storied columns and a wrap-around porch from which hung an American flag.

"Your uncle's house looks like a plantation," Ben said.

"It probably was at one point," Chris said.

The Jeep pulled up to the front of the mansion. Ben imagined a horse-drawn carriage making the same looping motion 200 years ago.

The front door of the house opened. Uncle Joseph stepped onto the porch. His shirt and slacks were pressed by humidity onto his stocky frame and his sandy hair was combed perfectly to the side. He wore thin-rimmed glasses and a thick, political grin. He waved robotically at the Jeep.

# CHAPTER 12

Uncle Joseph grinned and shook Chris' hand firmly; Uncle Joseph's political career taught him how to project confidence and dominance through an initial handshake. He titled his hand above Chris' and maintained focused, penetrating eye contact, which informed Chris that the boys had entered his domain. Uncle Joseph performed the same tactic on Ben, who felt intimidated.

"Welcome to the great state of West Virginia, gentlemen. Come on in," Uncle Joseph said. "My servants will grab your luggage from the car and put your bags in your rooms. Aunt Charlotte is on the back porch. She made some sweet tea for us."

Ben and Chris walked through the foyer and into the kitchen, which was larger than Ben's entire childhood home. It's granite countertops, massive island, and sparkling appliances implied modern elegance, as did the full bar on the edge of the island. The kitchen architecture featured thick, dark-wood beams, which projected strength and power rather than delicate humility.

"You have an amazing kitchen, Uncle Joe," Chris said.

"Well, thank you," Uncle Joseph said. "We installed our island last year. Damn thing's as big as Cuba!"

Uncle Joseph led the boys through the kitchen and onto the deck in the backyard. The dark wood patio led to a gravel path that ended in a gazebo tangled in grapevines. Aunt Charlotte stood next to the patio table, which was decorated with pitchers of sweet tea and appetizers.

Aunt Charlotte waved to the gentlemen as they appeared through the French doors. Her petite stature conveyed no sense of imposition. Her fluffed, blonde hair was pulled into a bun, which accentuated her sharp nose. She wore a flower-patterned apron over her blue dress. Aunt Charlotte kissed her husband on the cheek; the action spawned from habit rather than adoration.

Ben and Chris sat next to each other at the table, while Uncle Joseph and Aunt Charlotte sat opposite. Chris reached for a sweet tea pitcher, but a servant emerged with agility from the corner to pour the sweet tea into Chris' glass. The servant filled all four cups and returned to his post.

"Maybe this place still *is* a plantation," Ben whispered to Chris.

"I was thinking the same thing," Chris whispered back. "I mean, I haven't seen a white servant in my uncle's house yet."

Uncle Joseph eyed his servant until he reached his original corner. The servant received a nod of acknowledgment from his employer, but no word of gratitude. Uncle Joseph swiveled his head toward his table guests.

"Well, boys," Uncle Joseph said, "how has the drive been so far?"

"Very fun," Chris said. "We've seen lots of historic sites and we've eaten some decent food."

Uncle Joseph nodded his head in recognition. Aunt Charlotte followed her husband's gesture.

"I've never driven through any of these states until now," Ben said, "so I've enjoyed seeing the countryside. Driving through Montana was beautiful."

Uncle Joseph leaned forward and rested his elbows on the table.

"Montana?" Uncle Joseph said. "Seems like wasted space to me. If I became Governor of Montana, I'd turn the whole damn place into a coal mine. Or an oil field."

Ben leaned forward, mirroring Uncle Joseph's posture.

"Why? Montana is beautiful," Ben said. "Have you ever been there?"

"No, boy," Uncle Joseph said, laughing. "I've never bothered to visit those barren places out West: Montana, South Dakota, Wyoming, Colorado. Those places seem like deserts filled with Cowboys and Indians."

Ben eyed Chris to gauge his expression. Ben had trouble deciding whether Uncle Joseph was joking or if he actually felt this way about the country.

"What about the West Coast?" Ben asked. "Have you ever been there? California, Oregon, Washington?"

"No I have not," Uncle Joseph said. "The West Coast is full of liberals and hippies. Why the hell would I want to bother with those types of people?"

"Oregon is a fun place to visit," Ben said. "That's where

I'm from."

Uncle Joseph leaned back in his chair and propped his hands behind his head in a gesture of superiority.

"Ah, you're a West Coast boy yourself," Uncle Joseph said. "So you know exactly what I'm talking about. All liberals out there."

"Well, not necessarily," Ben said. "The major cities usually vote Democrat, but the rural areas on the West Coast vote Republican. Just like anywhere, really."

"Are you from the city or the country?" Uncle Joseph asked.

"I'm a city kid. Born and raised in downtown Portland," Ben said.

Uncle Joseph nodded, as if he assumed knowledge of every one of Ben's memories.

"So, you're a city boy," Uncle Joseph said. "What was it like growing up next to colored folk?"

Ben's eyes widened. He looked at the servant, who still stood in the shadowy corner.

"Excuse me?" Ben asked.

"Well, you lived in the city," Uncle Joseph said. "You probably lived next to colored folk and poor people. What was that like?"

Aunt Charlotte eyed Ben actively. She assessed his body language and determined that Ben was uncomfortable with the question; however, she thought her husband's question was logical. Chris, having grown up in this family, knew this question was coming; however, his West Coast college experience made him appalled at his uncle's judgmental attitude. Ben leaned back in his chair. The question made him angry, but he calmed himself with controlled breaths and steadied his pulse.

"Well, sir," Ben said, "I never thought about my lifestyle in those terms. To me, I grew up next to people with varied levels of income and with varieties of cultural backgrounds. This made me acknowledge my own cultural values while allowing me to experience and appreciate the cultural customs and values of other people. Overall, it made me a more well-rounded, open-minded person, which wouldn't have been possible had I grown up in a homogeneous environment, like I imagine this town to be."

Uncle Joseph looked at Ben with wide eyes. He felt shocked at Ben's audacity and sharp vocal tone. Chris suppressed a laugh, which manifested itself in a nostril flare. Aunt Charlotte appeared appalled, but she waited for her husband to express her ideas. She had been instructed by her husband to remain quiet when it came to political discussion because he did not want the public to view their household as ideologically divided. In the shadowy corner, the servant grinned with slight satisfaction.

"Now, Ben," Uncle Joseph said, "I'm not sure if you're aware, but I'm running for Governor of West Virginia."

"Good luck," Ben said, with spark in his voice.

"Thank you, but I won't need it," Uncle Joseph said. "You see, I'm running on the Republican ticket, and that's the ticket of West Virginia."

"Lucky for you," Ben said.

Uncle Joseph dismissed the comment and continued with his original thought.

"My reason in telling you this lies with the courtesy of making you aware of who you're talking to," Uncle Joseph said.

Ben thought of the bribe money in Chris' glove compartment. He glared at Uncle Joseph.

"Sir, I am fully aware of the kind of man you are," Ben said.

"Good," Uncle Joseph said.

Chris felt uncomfortable. He knew that his uncle was a corrupt individual; however, he was family. Chris knew that Ben's answers were just and he wanted to support his friend; however, he thought that Ben was creating a tense situation when he could have suppressed his beliefs for the sake of the group's tranquility. Chris started to perspire and, though it was humid, his sweat came from nerves. He shifted in his chair.

The servant emerged from the corner and receded into the kitchen. He returned seconds later with a fresh pitcher of sweet tea, which he placed on the table.

"Is there anything else I can do for you, sir?" the servant asked.

"As always, Terry: be invisible," Uncle Joseph said.

The servant nodded. He looked at Ben with understanding and returned to his shadowy corner.

The sun began to set behind the trees and the backyard light faded. Soon, the yard lights glowed warmly, though a breeze swirled through the open space. Uncle Joseph beckoned his servant to bring him a sweater. Ben and Chris felt comfortable as the temperature and humidity lessened, though they grew uncomfortable as the tension between Uncle Joseph's ideologies became more antagonizing. The thought of the money in the glove compartment weighed heavily on the boys' minds.

"So, Chris," Uncle Joseph said, "you graduated from

college. Although it wasn't an Ivy League school, a degree is still a necessary commodity. What will you do with it?"

"Well, Uncle Joe," Chris said, "I have a job at JP Morgan Chase on Wall Street, so I'll be working with money all day."

"Wall Street," Uncle Joseph said. "A prestigious job like that will lead to a good life and a good wife."

Chris laughed out of obligation. Ben smirked with sarcasm.

"And," Uncle Joseph continued, "that kind of prestige could lead you to a successful career in politics later on. When I win the Governor's seat, you can use the family name to your political advantage."

"I don't know if I'm cut out for politics," Chris said.

"Sure you are," Uncle Joseph said. "If you can work with money, you're made for politics."

Ben leaned forward in his chair. The patio lights illuminated his face.

"What does money have to do with creating policy for the greater good of humanity?" Ben asked.

Uncle Joseph grinned widely. The grin struck Ben as dubious.

"The American political system is all about money, boy," Uncle Joseph said. "It's a beautiful system. The best political system in the world."

Uncle Joseph leaned back in his chair. The light receded from his face, creating a heavy shadow.

"The man with the most money can buy power and influence in his community," Uncle Joseph continued. "And with that power and influence, he can earn more money, which he can use to purchase even more power and influence. This political system, boys, is cutthroat, but it favors the hard-working classes like myself. Damn, I love capitalism."

Chris looked around at his uncle's house. The monstrosity of a dwelling pushed Uncle Joseph's wealth on Chris' eyes; the mansion hardly suggested Uncle Joseph's hard-working mentality, but it did imply sheer riches, power, and influence.

"Do you think the American political system helps everyone to follow their pursuit of happiness?" Ben asked.

"Of course I do," Uncle Joseph said.

"Then how does it help poor people?" Ben asked. "How will you help impoverished West Virginians *if* you become Governor?"

"Poor people don't need my help or the help of the government," Uncle Joseph said. "Poor people are poor because they're lazy and don't want to work for their money. Everyone has a chance at the American Dream. It's just a matter of how hard you work."

Ben's eyes flared. He recalled the hard-working mentality that his mother and father both shared. He reflected briefly on the reason that his father enlisted in the military: it provided opportunities for hard work that would result in money for his family.

Yet, his family remained poor throughout his whole childhood. Ben's father joined the Marines to follow the legend of the American Dream: if someone works hard enough, they will grow rich and secure.

Instead, Ben's father died in his pursuit of the American Dream while fighting in the name of the country who supposedly supports that dream. This pursuit of riches, Ben thought, left his mother without anything to show for her husband's death, except a son following the road to poverty and desperation.

"The American Dream is just rhetoric to make poor people feel like they have a chance," Ben said.

Uncle Joseph eyed Ben and invited him to continue with smug interest.

"With politicians so focused on lining their own pockets instead of bettering the country for *all* people, it's no wonder why poor people remain poor. And with white politicians continuously instilling the values of white culture, it's no wonder why the majority of the poor population is the ethnic minority, both here and in the countries that the U.S. occupies with its guns."

"You're a pretty vicious wordsmith, boy," Uncle Joseph said. "What's your plan after college?"

Ben paused. He began to sweat with nerves at the question. He was so focused on battling ideological injustices that he neglected Uncle Joseph's original warning: he was speaking to the most powerful person in West Virginia.

"I don't have a plan yet," Ben said.

Uncle Joseph rolled his eyes.

"So, here you are defending the poor person's mentality, when, as it turns out, you have that same lazy mentality yourself," Uncle Joseph said.

The comment punched Ben in the stomach. His throat began to croak and he felt tears behind his eyes. He felt that Uncle Joseph's comment insulted his father and mother. And Ben recognized something else: maybe Uncle Joseph was right. Maybe Ben had no chance at finding a career, much less a job. Maybe Ben was destined for poverty.

Maybe Ben was just a lazy kid who paid for a college education with free government money because he could not afford to hold a full-time job on his own.

Ben's insecurity with his position on the socioeconomic totem pole finally manifested itself into a well of water that waited behind his eyes, ready to flow.

Ben controlled his breathing. He would not cry in front of this man. He refused to give him that sense of victory. Ben breathed in through the nose, and out through his mouth.

"Sir," Ben started, "do you believe that money makes you happy?"

"I am very happy, boy," Uncle Joseph said.

"If this big house, your cars, your dogs, and your servants were taken away from you, would you still be happy?" Ben said.

"You're asking me if I would be a happy poor person like yourself?" Uncle Joseph asked.

"Exactly," Ben said. "Is it your money and political prowess that fuels your happiness, or is it the moral and ethical person inside of you that makes you happy?"

Aunt Charlotte looked at her husband intently. She never thought that her husband might be unhappy, though she sensed her own hollow, empty persona on a daily basis.

Chris reflected on the question, a question which he and Ben had argued about for 3,000 miles. Now, Chris did not agree with Ben, but maybe he did not disagree either.

"That's a pretty deep question, young man," Uncle Joseph said. "I think we'll end on that note. Charlotte, let's head to bed. It's getting late and I know these boys have to leave very early in the morning."

"Thank you for the sweet tea," Ben said to Aunt Charlotte.

"You're welcome, gentlemen," Aunt Charlotte replied.

Uncle Joseph stood, half-bowed to the boys, and walked through his French doors into the kitchen. Aunt Charlotte followed his example in precise pantomime. Ben and Chris stood to follow, but the servant in the corner moved quickly toward them.

"You know, fellas," the servant said, "you're alright."

"Thank you, sir," Ben said. "And thanks for filling my glass with Aunt Charlotte's sweet tea. You didn't have to do that, you know."

"Sure I did," the servant said.

He turned to walk into the servant's door, but turned.

"And I'm glad you liked *my* sweet tea," the servant said. "Miss Charlotte's never made sweet tea in her life."

He turned and continued through the servant's door. Ben and Chris looked at each other and grinned. They walked into the kitchen and found it empty. They walked upstairs and entered a dim hallway. Ben turned left to his room and Chris turned right toward his.

Ben closed his door and sat on his bed. He looked at a mirror that stood across from him. He stared at his own face, which looked pallid and flustered. Then, he felt a surge of emotion erupt behind his eyes, a surge that had waited to emerge for over an hour. He started to cry.

He watched himself cry in the mirror and wondered why he was crying in the first place. *What emotion created these tears?* Ben thought. *Was it fear of insignificance? Or reminiscence of possibilities unfulfilled?* Ben found no answers in his self-interrogation.

Eventually, the sobbing subsided and he reached into his backpack for his own journal, but he noticed his father's notebook and removed that instead. He opened it to a page midway through the journal and began to read.

*July 16, 2005*

*Man, I wish I could hurry and finish this Marine deployment. I know I'm going to get paid well eventually, but I haven't seen nearly enough money to make this experience worth-while yet. I've sent all my money home to my wife. It isn't much, but at least it's enough to allow my son to play sports and for my wife to buy food.*

*I really hate all the violence I'm witnessing day-in and day-out. It feels like I see someone die in a brutal way every single day. And not my buddies in the Marines, but innocent civilians who just want to live their lives. I pray every day for an end to all war. I mean, this isn't even a war. It's an invasion.*

*We're a bunch of poor Americans aiming guns at poor Iraqis and we expect them to welcome us with open arms, but instead, they act logically and they try to fight against us. And our officers are shocked by this notions. What a bunch of idiots.*

*I have an idea: maybe instead of aiming guns at innocent Iraqi families under the guise of help, how about we actually help them and approach them with peace and kindness. How about we collaborate through education and cultural understanding, instead of shooting people and creating even more instability in an environment of chaos. Oh, because then our government couldn't control the oil prices through a gun barrel. And back to the root of all problems in this world: power, money, and influence. Damn, I should become President.*

*David E.*

Ben closed the journal. His eyes were dry and he found a smile on his face when he looked in the mirror. He felt emboldened by the fact that he had the same social perceptions as his father. Ben felt mystified that his father was able to instill a sense of social justice in his son, even though their time together was brief.

He replaced his father's journal in its backpack pocket and climbed in bed prepared to sleep. As his mind quieted, he heard voices through the wall. The voices were faint enough that Ben could choose to ignore them, but they were articulate enough that Ben could eavesdrop. He chose the journalistic option.

"Why can't you just be cheerful, Joe?" Aunt Charlotte said.

"I just have a lot of pressure to win this election from outside influences," Uncle Joseph said.

"You're so wrapped up in your political agenda that you've forgotten how to have compassion," Aunt Charlotte said.

"Well, when this money comes in, I'll be that much closer to a guaranteed victory," Uncle Joseph said. "And when I win this election, I'll be happy."

A television turned on in the next room, which drowned the faint voices completely, so Ben closed his eyes and faded toward sleep. Suddenly, his mind raced. He felt his pulse quicken. *When this money comes in, I'll be that much closer to a guaranteed victory.* Ben thought about the cash in Chris' glove compartment. A sudden fear gripped him.

He shut his eyes tighter and drifted into sleep.

# CHAPTER 13

Chris awoke early and strolled downstairs in basketball shorts and a light cotton shirt. Even though the morning temperature read cold, the humidity gave the house a layer of heat. Uncle Joseph sat on a barstool in the kitchen with a cup of Earl Grey tea beside him. He folded his *Wall Street Journal* in half and placed it on the kitchen island, lowering his glasses to read an article about the nation's stagnant unemployment rate. He heard Chris' footsteps, but continued reading.

"Well, good morning, nephew," Uncle Joseph said, without looking up from his newspaper. "How'd you sleep?"

"I slept fine, Uncle," Chris said.

Chris rubbed his eyes sleepily. He squinted as a sun beam shot through the half-open wooden blinds.

"Would you like some coffee, Chris?" Uncle Joseph said.

"Yes, please," Chris said.

Uncle Joseph beckoned toward his servant, who moved

from his corner with efficiency. He poured the black coffee into a large, elegant mug and placed it on the kitchen island near a bar stool across from Uncle Joseph. Chris thanked him and sat, while the servant returned to the corner of the room without acknowledgement from the homeowner.

"You know, you're going to have to wake up much earlier than this when you begin that Wall Street job with JP Morgan Chase," Uncle Joseph said to Chris. "Heck, you're going to be up before the sun. You're going to have to do your research before you even think about breakfast."

"I will, sir," Chris said. "I'm a hard worker."

"I know it, nephew," Uncle Joseph said. "And, you'll have to find yourself some inside connections with the companies you're trading. That'll sure give you a competitive edge."

"I'm not exactly allowed to do that," Chris said. "In fact, I'm pretty sure that's illegal."

"That's business," Uncle Joseph said.

Chris paused and looked at his uncle with perplexed compassion.

"Well, at any rate," Uncle Joseph continued, "I'm awfully proud of you. You're headed off toward a bright future full of money and influence. Just keep looking out for yourself and you'll be alright."

"Thanks, Uncle," Chris said.

"And I'm just glad that you found a career that's going to make you money," Uncle Joseph said. "Unlike your friend, Ben, who doesn't seem to have amounted to much success."

"He'll find something that he enjoys and he'll be happy. I'm not worried," Chris said.

"Well, that's good. Life without money is no life for a

Morgan man; I'll tell you that," Uncle Joseph said.

He returned his gaze to the financial newspaper and immersed himself into another article about political campaign contributions.

Chris watched his uncle. He noticed how his uncle's eyes narrowed, which created creases in his forehead that left a lasting imprint on his face from years of unhappiness. He noticed his uncle's eyes; the spark that Chris remembered from childhood had now vanished from his uncle's face. Instead, Uncle Joseph's face was lined with corruption and emptiness.

Chris turned as he heard a floorboard creak behind him. Ben walked down the stairs and entered the kitchen. He sat on a bar stool next to Chris.

"Good morning," Ben said.

"Hey, man," Chris said.

Uncle Joseph continued to read his newspaper and drowned the chatter between the two friends. Once he finished his article, he looked toward Ben.

"So, you boys are headed to Philadelphia today, correct?" Uncle Joseph said.

"We are," Chris said. "We'll spend a day there and then move on to New York City: our final stop."

"Now, Chris, I understand why you're going to New York," Uncle Joseph said, "but I can't figure out why you're moving there, Ben. I mean, you're moving all the way across the country, and for what?"

Ben pondered the question. He had thought about his reasoning through the duration of the road trip, and still he felt unsure about his answer. He knew that his choice to move to New York City felt right, but he could not provide a logical reason for his decision.

An analytical personality like Uncle Joseph would accept only logic, not feelings of spontaneity. Ben looked at Chris for reassurance. He felt immersed in insecurity, which amplified with his thoughts of stupidity for his spontaneous decision to move to New York. He returned his glance to Uncle Joseph and attempted to project confidence, though he felt his voice quake.

"Well, I wanted a change of scenery," Ben said. "I wanted to move to a place where I could utilize my public relations training and implement my writing skills. New York City provides opportunities for that. It's a legendary city that thrives on creativity and diversity, so I figured I'd check it out."

Ben paused for a moment and gauged Uncle Joseph's reaction by reading his facial features and body language. Uncle Joseph looked unimpressed with the answer. Ben felt the need to prove himself to the most powerful man in West Virginia, so he continued.

"And my mom lives in New York City," Ben said.

Uncle Joseph's eyebrows raised, signifying that he accepted this as a passable answer.

"Well, why didn't you say so in the first place?" Uncle Joseph said. "What does your mother do in the City?"

"I'm not really sure," Ben said. "I haven't talked with her in a while. She was pursuing a Broadway acting career last time I checked."

Uncle Joseph frowned and returned his focus to the newspaper.

○   ○   ○

Chris closed the Jeep's trunk and Ben shoved his backpack into its usual slot in the back seat. Chris hugged Aunt Charlotte and shook hands rigidly with Uncle Joseph. Aunt Charlotte gave Chris a plate of baked pastries that she claimed to have made, though Chris suspected that the servant had produced the delicious treats.

Ben shook Uncle Joseph's hand, a moment he had dreaded since the previous night's conversation over sweet tea. Uncle Joseph dominated the handshake with a firm grip and piercing eye contact. Though Ben tried to project confidence, he felt himself cower.

For the first time in his life, Ben was intimidated by a man's title rather than by a man's character, a sentiment which grew from his own insecurity with his own title: the unemployed poor vagabond.

Ben sat in the driver's seat, while Chris accepted the passenger chair. The Jeep roared with ferocity as it started. It reversed, and then pulled forward with anger. It tore through the dirt road and dashed onto the pavement. Excitedly, it sprinted forward toward the majesty of the Blue Ridge Mountains and away from the tyranny of Uncle Joseph's plantation.

The boys remained quiet in the cockpit of the Jeep. No music played. No words were exchanged.

Chris felt slightly embarrassed about his uncle's antagonizing attitude toward Ben, but he recognized the blunt truth in his uncle's analysis. After all, Ben was unemployed and the decision to move to New York City was foolishly whimsical.

Chris could not fathom a life without a secure job. In

fact, Chris recognized that he needed a job that provided an excess amount of money because this gave him a sense of worth. He found confidence when he compared his annual salary to that of other people his age; he often compared himself to his peers in an attempt to assign personal accomplishment to his own self-worth. He recognized that his identity was tied with his rank in social status.

Yet, he recognized that Ben's philosophy about happiness was gradually taking hold of his own thoughts. Maybe Chris needed to place a higher percentage of his self-worth on creativity, virtue, and simplicity. He tried to delineate this paradox: how could he gain wealth and status, yet strive for happiness with simplicity and altruism?

Meanwhile, Ben stared out the front window. The Blue Ridge Mountains enveloped his focus. The trees hung low, yet towered overhead. In front of Ben, the closest trees appeared as vibrant green, but as the trees blended into the forest, they faded into a shade of hazy blue.

Ben recalled the leaders of the transcendentalist writing style and wondered how much the Walden Pond natural landscape influenced their abilities as wordsmiths. His thoughts drifted specifically toward Ralph Waldo Emerson, his namesake.

Ben absorbed the beauty of the unfamiliar Southern landscape. He felt the humidity embrace the cockpit and he watched the trees remain stagnant in the breeze's absence. Suddenly, he felt at peace. The momentary dedication to silent observance allowed nature to bring him happiness during a period of self-doubt. His momentary drop in self-worth became obsolete as the Blue Ridge Mountains calmed Ben's attitude by simple presence.

Suddenly, Chris' phone rang. Ben's meditative concentration broke and Chris snapped from his trance. He reached for his phone, looked at the unfamiliar phone number, and lifted it toward his ear.

"Hello?" Chris said.

"Hello," said a sophisticated man's voice. "May I please speak with Christopher Morgan?"

"This is him," Chris said.

"Ah, hello, Mr. Morgan," the voice said. "I'm Stephen O'Connell with JP Morgan Chase. How are you doing this morning?"

Chris' nerves felt electrified. His demeanor shifted from casual road trip journeyman to business class executive.

"I'm doing just fine, sir," Chris said. "What can I do for you?"

"Well, Mr. Morgan," the voice said, "I have some unfortunate news, I'm afraid."

Chris felt his breath quicken and his throat began to close. His hands began to shake; his foot tapped involuntarily.

"What kind of news?" Chris asked, his voice shaking.

"Well, you see," the voice said, "due to unfortunate business circumstances and general economic recession, we've decided to eliminate your position."

"What do you mean, exactly," Chris said, though he was fully aware of the man's meaning.

"Mr. Morgan, we no longer need your services with our company," the man said. "I'm sorry."

"But, I haven't even started the job," Chris said.

"We're aware, which is why we wanted to inform you of this unfortunate circumstance as soon as we could," the man said.

Chris' panic manifested itself through an angry vocal tone.

"What about my apartment in the City?" Chris snapped.

"Well, you can't live there, of course," the man said. "Our firm has a lease on the entire floor of the loft complex."

Chris began to cry, but he held his tears tightly to his eyelids and suppressed the sounds that yearned to escape through his vocal chords.

"I'm sorry, Mr. Morgan," the man said. "We do wish you the best of luck in the future, and we'll keep your name in our files in case another position that fits your talents opens up in the years to come. Good day, sir."

Chris could not respond to the man. He simply ended the call and dropped his phone to the floor.

Ben looked at Chris and noticed his tears, and then Chris began to sob. Tears poured from his eyes in an endless stream of emotion. He covered his face with his hands to muffle the wailing sounds, but it only amplified them. Chris' sobs filled the Jeep's cockpit.

Ben empathized with Chris' emotions; Ben received the same phone call only days earlier. Ben remembered his momentary battle with panic and helplessness, but he noticed a difference between Chris' situation and his own. Ben did not equate his self-worth with his career title; however, Chris' self-image *was* his job title.

"I'm ruined!" Chris shouted.

The Jeep surged forward with ferocity, and then lagged to a sluggish pace. It pulled into the right lane with anticipation of a quick exit from the highway.

"I'm so sorry, man," Ben said with sincerity.

Chris' sobs began to subside, though he took short, choppy breaths that seemed to only inhale without release.

"How can they fire me when I haven't even started my job?" Chris wailed.

"It's not fair, Chris," Ben said. "That's the economy for you."

"It's not the economy's fault. It's mine! I wasn't good enough," Chris said.

Ben did not know how to respond. He knew that Chris was in pain and that his thoughts would be irrational based on his emotional state. Ben knew because he had the same thoughts when he received a phone call like that from Portland Public Relations.

"Trust me, Chris. I've been there," Ben said. "It doesn't feel good, but you have to know that the reason they couldn't let you work for them is because their business isn't doing well. It's not your fault. It has nothing to do with you."

"You don't know how I'm feeling, Ben!" Chris shouted. "I just did four years of college for nothing! I was supposed to be a financial executive, and then become C.E.O., and then become a millionaire, and then get married to the finest girl in New York, and then run for Governor, and then President! Now that plan is ruined."

Ben focused on the Blue Ridge Mountains. The sun began to rise higher over the hills, so the forest shifted from hazy blue to deep marine.

"I was supposed to be Chris Morgan: 22-year-old financial professional and soon-to-be millionaire," Chris said. "Now, I'm Chris Morgan: nothing."

Chris turned his head and stared out the window. He focused on each individual tree, which looked greener than the entirety of the forest. Chris felt the weight of failure engulf him; time seemed to slow down and speed up simultaneously. Contrarily, time seemed to flow smoothly for Ben, who gazed at the rolling blue forest, an ocean of mountains.

The journeymen remained silent for miles. The Jeep passed through the handle of Maryland, which prompted Ben to take a photograph of the state's entrance sign. He did so while driving, so the quality did not suit his usual expectations.

Ben rested the camera on the dashboard in front of the steering wheel; the lens faced outward toward the road. Soon, Maryland faded into the rear view mirror and Ben snapped a photograph of the *Welcome to Pennsylvania* road sign.

Then, Ben clicked his camera's trigger again and looked at his camera's viewing screen. The second blue sign read: *Mason-Dixon Line*.

"Chris, did you see that sign?" Ben asked, interrupting the silent environment.

"No." Chris said.

"We just crossed the Mason-Dixon Line," Ben said. "Think about how many escaped slaves did the same thing. Except they did it on foot, through swamps, in the dark, with hunting dogs on their trail. And the threat of death by whipping on their minds the entire journey."

He waited for a usual response from Chris, but he received no acknowledgement from his friend, who remained in a state of desolation in the passenger seat.

Ben thought about an escaped slave, like Frederick Douglass, making a daring escape. What courage he must have possessed in order to overcome that intense fear that suppressed so many people for so many years.

Then, he thought about the concept of slavery and felt adamant that the institution was terrible, produced from an idea that monetary value supersedes moral obligation and maintained through years of ingrained hatred that passed through generations of rich, white, Americans: the writers of history.

"Do you think that slaves were happy?" Ben asked.

"I don't know," Chris said with muffled effort.

"I'll bet the slaves were happier than the slave owners," Ben said.

Chris turned to Ben with a facial expression of disagreement.

"And how do you figure that?" Chris asked.

"Well," Ben said, "don't get me wrong. Being a slave in the South would have been terrible. Whippings. Separated from your family and sold as property instead of employed as a human. No civil rights. I get that. But think about how unhappy a slave owner must have been."

Chris' face twisted into a perplexed expression and he looked at Ben with curious eyes.

"What do you mean?" Chris asked.

"A slave owner had to fall asleep at night with the guilt of stealing people's freedoms, with the guilt of whipping people that he saw every day, with the guilt of striping away everything that a person was and morphing someone into some-*thing*. Furthermore, a slave owner's sole goal was profit, and living a life that only strives for more money will drive a man to do terrible things, and that rots a man's soul."

"Maybe you're right," Chris said with more enthusiasm. "If a person only lives for money, he'll do awful things, but will he care about how he affects other people if he's obtaining his financial goal?"

Ben thought as he looked out the window. The yellow lines that separated the highway lanes seemed to move to the North in the direction that escaped slaves would have travelled.

"Every man has a conscience, Chris. At least slaves went to bed at night with the freedom of conscience," Ben said. "The slave owner was imprisoned by his. And rightly so."

Chris nodded in agreement and continued his solace as he stared out of the side window. The boys drove in silence for miles. Not even the radio interrupted the glassy atmosphere.

Ahead, the Jeep crossed over the Appalachian Mountains and connected with Highway 76: The Pennsylvania Turnpike. Ben's mind raced.

"Do you suppose it's called Highway 76 because it runs into Philadelphia?" Ben asked.

"I don't know?" Chris said. "Why would 76 and Philadelphia have anything to do with each other?"

"July 4th, 1776, Chris!" Ben shouted. "The year that the Declaration of Independence was written and signed and read in Philadelphia. Tomorrow marks the 236th anniversary of that monumental occasion in the history of the United States of America."

"Wow, Ben, you're right," Chris said.

"I know it's only July Third," Ben said, "but Happy

Independence Day."

"Why not wait until tomorrow, July Fourth?" Chris asked.

"Because," Ben said. "It's *your* Independence Day. Now you're not confined to the shackles of a major Wall Street firm. Now, you can do whatever you want."

"You and me both, buddy," Chris said. "We're both happily unemployed college graduates, just like everyone else. A lot of good that Declaration of Independence did for guys like us, 236 years later."

"We'll be just fine, Chris," Ben said. "Let's see what Philly has to offer."

The Jeep crested the highway and saw Philadelphia skyscrapers on the horizon. The sun hung low behind them, but enough daylight remained for the Jeep to reach the city. It exited the highway and pulled into the hotel parking lot in downtown. Ben removed the keys from the ignition and the Jeep exhaled. Ben exhaled as well, while Chris continued to mope in the passenger seat.

"Let's unpack," Ben said. "I need a beer."

"I'm ruined," Chris mumbled. "I need something stronger."

"Come on, buddy," Ben said. "Let's go grab a celebratory beer in honor of our own, unique Independence Day."

Chris looked at Ben with an expression of plunging depression; Chris' face exuded desperation. Ben was worried. His friend and co-pilot looked unstable.

# CHAPTER 14

Chris sat on the curb outside of the Revolution Hotel as the sun dropped below the skyscrapers. Ben carried his own backpack and one of Chris' suitcases into the hotel's main lobby. He asked the hotel's front desk to check in under a reservation for Chris Morgan, which worked. Chris' Wall Street firm had neglected to cancel the hotel reservation in Philadelphia, a corporate oversight that thrilled Ben's tired eyes.

When Ben emerged from the hotel, he found Chris sulking. Clouds covered the sunlight outside and Chris stared into the dark pavement with a blank expression. He felt a sensation of total failure. He feared the conversation with his parents because he knew his father would be disappointed in his son's diminished social stature. Chris had no backup plan.

A feeling of complete hopelessness enveloped his entire body. He began to shake. His nerves tightened and his breathing quickened. He felt his throat begin to close.

As he stared at the pavement, his peripheral vision became blurry and he felt his consciousness dwindle, which sent panic through his nervous system. He felt his heart exploding through his chest. The hotel began to fade away, and then the cars in the parking lot, until the only feature in Chris' focus was the blurry pavement. He felt as if he did not exist. And he felt good about that.

"We're all set here at the Revolution Hotel," Ben said.

Chris snapped his head toward Ben. A sudden awareness gripped him and his breathing gradually progressed toward regularity. Ben opened the Jeep's trunk flap and unloaded one round of luggage.

Eventually, Chris left his post on the curb and helped Ben with a suitcase and a trunk. The boys took the elevator to floor 17 and deposited their luggage. Chris sat on the nearest bed and drooped his face.

"Alright, dude," Ben said with optimistic authority.

"What?" Chris asked.

"Stand up," Ben said. "We're going downstairs to the hotel bar to drink one beer and eat some fries. Don't make me go alone."

"Fine," Chris said. "I guess we can see if the JP Morgan Chase business credit card still works."

"I like that attitude!" Ben shouted. "If they forgot to cancel it, then it's their fault for letting you go. You would have been smart enough to cancel it, but they were dumb enough to close your position, so let's take them for all their corporate asses are worth."

Ben paused and smiled.

"Or at least enough for two beers and some fries," Ben said.

Finally, Chris forced a laugh. Ben smiled and hoped that Chris' mental state was improving. The elevator stopped and the boys exited into the lobby and turned left toward the hotel bar. People packed the establishment, but the boys found open barstools near the beer tap handles.

Ben ordered a local Philadelphia porter, while Chris ordered an East Coast Pale Ale; trying local brews at each stop had been customary at this point in their journey. Ben ordered a small basket of fries. He asked the bartender why so many people attended the bar area this evening. He told them that people from all over the country come to Philadelphia during the Fourth of July in order to rediscover the roots of the United States of America.

After their pint glasses emptied, the boys attempted to pay with Chris' JP Morgan Chase company credit card, which worked. Chris wanted to take Wall Street for every penny he could, a motivation cultivated from vengeance, or justice. At this point in the journey, Ben had little money left from his college job, so the free drinks enhanced his financial security, if only by a few dollars.

When they arrived at their hotel room, Ben opened his journal and sat on his bed and began to write about his day. Chris walked onto the balcony and sat in a chair and overlooked the city. Though the sun was gone, the city felt bright. Street lights and Independence Day celebration preparations lit the environment, as did the influx of people that bustled along the streets below Chris.

He wondered what living in a city this large would feel like, especially if he had a lot of money and status, which he would have accumulated if JP Morgan Chase had not fired him. He began to question his future and self-worth again.

*Why didn't someone else take a pay cut?*

Chris gazed at Philadelphia from a downward perspective. He did not know who he was now, or what he would become. He knew the skillset that he possessed, but he could not attach his talents or his morality to his personal identity; for some ingrained reason, only a career title could describe his personal identity.

He blamed his Morgan family lineage and ideology for attaching his self-worth to his social stature. As he looked down on Philadelphia, he had no title; thus, he felt that he had no identity.

The hotel room lights dimmed. Soon, Chris heard Ben's light snores. Chris contemplated leaving the balcony and sleeping, but his mind raced too actively and his thoughts about his own self-worth needed more exploration, no matter how dark they seemed at this moment.

He stood from his chair and approached the railing. He looked down at the street, which provoked an uncomfortable sensation along his spine; vertigo rushed through his body and mind, which made him stagger slightly and grasp the guardrail tightly.

Then, he stared straight forward. The City of Brotherly Love expanded and faded before him.

o o o

Ben awoke early. He rolled over and noticed that Chris' bed was empty and perfectly made, like it went unused during the night. Ben stood and looked in the bathroom, but he did not see Chris. Then, he noticed that the balcony door was open.

He stepped onto the deck and saw Chris sleeping in the padded, wicker chair. His neck kinked to one side.

Ben tapped the wicker chair hard with his foot and Chris' head snapped upwards. He looked around in bewilderment, as he did not recall falling asleep on a deck in Philadelphia. His clothes felt damp with morning dew. He saw the sun rising and heard the buzz of morning traffic below. Then, he spun his whole body around and saw Ben, who leaned against the doorframe and laughed at Chris' confusion.

"Good morning, sunshine," Ben said.

"Did I fall asleep out here?" Chris asked.

"It appears so, mopey," Ben said. "How are you feeling this morning?"

"Better," Chris said. "My neck hurts though. And I'm cold."

"I bet," Ben said. "Go get ready for the day. We have a lot of exploring to do."

"What do you mean?" Chris asked. "We have to drive to New York today."

"Do we?" Ben asked. "And why do we have to arrive in New York so soon?"

"I have to start," Chris began.

"Start what?" Ben asked. "A new job?"

Chris turned and looked at the sun rising over the city. His eyes sunk.

"I guess not," Chris said.

"We might as well stay in Philly today and head to New York tomorrow. There's nothing waiting for us there," Ben said.

Ben smiled assuringly. Chris felt amazed at Ben's optimism in the face of unemployment, an emotion that felt foreign to Chris.

"Besides, it's the Fourth of July!" Ben shouted. "We might as well feel independent from corporate America in the city that pioneered the philosophy of American independence."

Chris showered and dressed quickly. His brain forced him to feel ashamed of his absent job title, but he powered through his morning routine with vigor; somehow, Ben's positive attitude motivated him to explore Philadelphia with a newfound exuberance for adventure. The boys took the elevator to the lobby and approached the front desk.

"Ben, what are you doing?" Chris whispered.

"Trust me," Ben said.

The hotel employee addressed Ben with a glance of acknowledgement.

"Excuse me, sir," Ben said. "We would like to extend our stay by one night, if that's possible."

The employee nodded and checked the hotel schedule for the upcoming evening. He smiled with reassurance.

"One more night," he said. "You gentlemen are all set. Will this be on the same credit card as last night?"

"Yes it will," Chris said with a smile.

The hotel employee nodded and the boys turned and exited the hotel through the revolving doors. They strolled down Market Street and dodged crowds of people who hustled to their destinations and appointments in semi-formal, East Coast attire. Some walkers appeared as tourists, as made evident by their maps, fanny packs, and absent Philadelphia accents.

Ben and Chris felt like tourists, but their appearance made that fact less obvious than other tour groups. Secretly,

Chris lamented the tourists' attire because they appeared unprofessional, but he knew that he appeared the same way. He wanted to dress in business attire and walk the streets with a financial purpose, but he knew that his dream may never manifest. He wanted people to look at him and be impressed and intimidated by his professional attributes.

The sun burned all clouds from the sky and created a bright, hot atmosphere. Humidity began to linger. Chris' eyes hid behind dignified sunglasses, while Ben squinted and regretted his decision to leave his sunglasses behind in Oregon after college graduation.

Eventually, the boys reached 6th Street and turned to walk through Independence National Historical Park. A thick crowd gathered in front of Independence Hall, so Ben and Chris pushed their way through and neared the front of the mob.

"What are all these people waiting for?" Chris asked.

"Fourth of July fireworks, maybe," Ben said.

"In the morning?" Chris asked rhetorically. "I doubt it."

Ben looked toward the front of the crowd and saw a banner.

"It looks like they're doing a reenactment of Thomas Jefferson's original reading of the Declaration of Independence," Ben said.

"Why here?" Chris asked.

"Independence Hall is where the Founding Fathers signed it," Ben said. "And on the Fourth of July, a crowd gathered to hear it read before they sent it to King George in England."

Chris nodded in acceptance of the facts. He looked around at the swelling crowd. A bead of sweat dripped from his forehead.

"Hey, Ben," Chris said, "I don't know how long I can wait in this heat. When do you think it starts?"

Speakers bellowed from the front of the crowd. A man in a blue suit appeared on the stage in front of Independence Hall. He approached the podium and spoke into the microphone with poise.

He gave a typical introductory speech, which included the thanking of the crowd and the Mayor of Philadelphia, who was seated on stage in a prominent location. Then, a man dressed as Thomas Jefferson in Revolutionary Era attire strode calmly onto the stage. He approached the microphone, adjusted his three-cornered hat, and unraveled a scroll. The crowd cheered wildly. He spoke slowly and eloquently.

"When in the Course of human events," the man preached, "it becomes necessary for one people to dissolve the political bands which have connected them with another, and to assume among them the powers of the earth, the separate and equal station to which the Laws of Nature and of Nature's God entitle them, a decent respect to the opinions of mankind requires that they should declare the causes which impel them to the separation."

Ben looked at Chris with historical excitement. He weaved through the crowd. Chris followed until the boys stood in front of the podium.

Independence Hall stood strong in the background; its red-bricked exterior projected Revolutionary ideals. The tower, which used to hold the Liberty Bell, spiraled upward to the clock, which read *9:16 a.m.* Ben stood in awe of the spoken word of Thomas Jefferson.

"We hold these truths to be self-evident, that all men are created equal, that they are endowed by their Creator with certain unalienable Rights, among these are Life, Liberty, and the pursuit of Happiness."

The crowd erupted. The iconic lines penned by Benjamin Franklin and spoken by Thomas Jefferson fueled the crowd's patriotism. The Independence Day atmosphere sizzled in the hot morning sun. When the speaker completed each paragraph, the crowd's energy rose and manifested with shouts.

Finally, the speaker completed his reading of the Declaration of Independence. The crowd applauded and the speaker returned to his seat on the stage. Then, the Mayor of Philadelphia approached the podium and thanked the group for celebrating the birthplace of the United States.

Ben and Chris maneuvered through the mass of people. They passed the Liberty Bell and Ben took a photograph through the glass window. As they reached the edge of the crowd, they walked toward open space.

They approached the entrance to an old cemetery. Ben read the sign, which was carved in stone and weathered by wind. Though faded, the date informed Ben that this was a Revolutionary War cemetery, so he entered. Chris followed.

After perusing through the graveyard's aisles, Ben noticed an historical marker near a flat gravestone. The engravings on the flat grave marker were weathered and illegible, but the historical marker informed Ben of the grave's significance.

"Chris," Ben said, "check this out. It's Benjamin Franklin's grave!"

"That's incredible," Chris said. "This is the most

intelligent person that ever lived in the United States."

Ben paid a silent tribute to his personal namesake. Since learning about Benjamin Franklin in the fifth grade, Ben possessed an admiration of the man's intellect and ability to influence the world in a positive way.

After observing the gravestones of a few more signers of the Declaration of Independence and the United States Constitution, the boys left the cemetery and returned to the city. They turned on 2nd Street and discussed their growing appetite and thirst.

They entered City Tavern. The host led the boys through the main bar and to the patio seating area. The old brick building appeared authentic, with its faded wood floors and uneven architecture. Ben looked at a menu and read that City Tavern was founded in 1773. John Adams, Benjamin Franklin, and Thomas Jefferson ate and drank in the tavern during their time in Philadelphia.

Ben and Chris both ordered a local ale because they assumed that the Founding Fathers drank ale when they attended City Tavern.

Ben looked around at the building and the grounds. Franklin, Jefferson, and Adams probably had in-depth political discussions and arguments while drinking ale at this tavern during the roasting summers that plagued the Continental Congress; many of those arguments formed the theories and ideals in the Declaration of Independence and the Constitution.

"I'll bet that Ben Franklin got drunk at this tavern and started bashing the absurd policies of King George," Ben said. "Then, Thomas Jefferson agreed and advised a course of action. John Adams provided the legal theory that these idea-men needed. And here we are today."

"And it's all thanks to ale," Chris said.

"I would love to have been a part of those drunken discussions between the Founding Fathers at this tavern," Ben said.

"I'll bet that this is where they came up with that phrase: Life, Liberty, and the Pursuit of Happiness," Chris said.

Ben sipped his ale and pondered the thought.

"Do you think the U.S. Founding Fathers were really happy?" Ben asked.

"Of course," Chris said. "Why wouldn't they be?"

"Lots of reasons," Ben said.

"Like what?" Chris asked. "They were rich, smart, and founded a country. What more do you need to be happy?"

"Sure, they were rich," Ben said. "But during the American Revolution, they didn't know that the United States would *actually* materialize. Technically, they were committing treason against England. If the Colonists lost the war, the Founding Fathers would have died painfully."

Ben paused to catch his breath and take a drink. Chris waited patiently, as he anticipated Ben's continuing rant about history, a pattern that had emerged throughout their friendship's formation.

"Also, just because they were rich didn't mean they had status. English nobles looked at these people like they were dirt because they didn't live in England. And, these guys were so busy with their actual jobs and politics that they barely had time to spend with their families."

Again, Ben paused to formulate his thoughts and to wait for recognition that Chris was following his line of thought. Chris nodded, which signaled Ben to continue.

"Ben Franklin spent years in France with women other than his wife. Thomas Jefferson had a baby with one of his slaves. And John Adams was perpetually miserable with stress as a lawyer and statesman."

Ben took a drink of ale and continued.

"Plus, they lived during a time when slavery was acceptable and the destruction of Native American society was the norm," Ben said. "Most of the Founding Fathers made their money on the work of slaves. Think about the moral burden those aspects of their lives would produce."

Chris looked down at his ale and took a large gulp. He leaned back in his chair and smiled at Ben's enjoyment of this historical analysis.

"We idealize these men for founding America," Ben continued, "even though millions of Native Americans were already living on this land and had been for thousands of years. Are our Founding Fathers worth this glorification?"

"Absolutely," Chris said. "Look at the money, power, and influence these guys had."

"And they used that power and influence to write a line that discusses Life, Liberty, and the Pursuit of Happiness," Ben said. "But, did they intend for those ingrained rights to apply to all people?"

"Well, I guess not," Chris said. "Mostly just rich, white men. I mean, women couldn't vote, black people were enslaved, Native Americans were dying of Westward Expansion, and poor people were imprisoned with debt and dying by fighting in the Revolutionary War."

"That's a solid point, Chris," Ben said. "You didn't see any rich, white guys fighting on the frontlines. Actually, you still don't. My dad was the perfect example. Rich guys make the policy from safe offices and they force the poor soldiers to carry out their dirty work."

Chris finished his ale and ordered another round for the table.

"What did they mean by the Pursuit of Happiness, anyway?" Chris asked.

"Actually, the original draft of the Declaration of Independence described the Pursuit of Property, based on John Locke's political theory," Ben said, "but Thomas Jefferson edited it to read *Happiness*."

"That's weird," Chris said. "Having acres of land wouldn't necessarily make me happier. I don't see the correlation."

"Rich men owned acres of property during the Revolutionary era," Ben said. "The more land you owned, the more crops you could grow. Or, the more crops you could force your slaves to grow and cultivate. Back then, land also gave a man his voting rights and enhanced his social status."

"Just like money does today, huh?" Chris said.

"Land and status was the dream of the rich white men who founded our country," Ben said.

Chris created frost designs with the dew on the side of his pint glass.

"I think it was the *pursuit* of this dream that made our Founding Fathers happy more so than the actual acreage of land or the monetary value associated with it," Chris said.

"Just like the *pursuit* of freedom probably gave American slaves happiness," Ben said. "Like Frederick Douglass. He held on to the hope that one day he could pursue freedom, and he became an incredibly influential statesman by pursuing his dream."

Chris lifted his eyes to the single cloud that floated in the blue Philadelphia skyline.

"Maybe I just need to figure out what my life's ultimate dream is," Chris said. "Even if I don't reach it, maybe the act of pursuing it will make me happy, rather than the act of receiving gobs of money."

Ben smiled at Chris' newfound revelation. He lifted his ale glass and motioned for Chris to do the same.

"It's amazing what a pint of ale will do for the mind," Ben said.

"And the soul," Chris said.

The boys paid for their tavern bill and returned to their hotel. They strolled into the entryway and Chris pressed the elevator button.

As they waited for the elevator to arrive, Ben noticed a pretty blonde girl checking in at the front desk. The elevator rang and the girl turned and stepped into the light.

"Lucy?" Ben said.

"Ben? I never thought I'd see you again!" Lucy said.

"I felt the same way," Ben said.

Chris stood awkwardly in the elevator and held the door.

"What are you doing here?" Lucy asked.

"We're staying in Philly for one more night, and then we're headed into New York," Ben said.

"That's our plan, too. We're leaving here midafternoon tomorrow for the City," Lucy said. "We're going to stay with Mary Anne's brother."

"Hey, guys," Chris said. "I'm going upstairs to go to sleep. I slept outside in a wicker chair last night and I need some good rest. See you later, Ben."

Chris let the elevator door close. He dreaded returning to the room alone. Though he had an adventurous day, he still felt lost without the prospect of a prestigious job. And seeing Ben with a new woman gave Chris a new sense of inferiority.

*Maybe Ben has something figured out that I don't*, Chris thought. *Maybe I do need to find a purpose that will make me happy that doesn't involve money. But, I love the idea of making money.*

Ben watched the elevator door close and he returned his gaze to Lucy. They moved their conversation to the lobby armchairs.

They talked about their road trips thus far. Then, their conversation shifted to a more personal level and they began to discuss their family. Lucy told Ben about her highest ambitions and dreams of serving people in any way possible because she wanted to play a role in curbing the injustices that she saw in the world.

Ben could feel her intelligence and altruism exude from every word. Her beauty and passion made Ben's heart flutter. He never felt this type of true connection with Samantha. He never admired someone's heart and caring spirit more than in this moment. Ben felt connected on a deeper level.

Ben looked at his watch. Two hours had passed since they began their conversation. He wrote down Lucy's phone number and promised to call her in a few days once he was settled in New York.

Even though Ben did not want to end their talk here, he recognized that he needed sleep before the final leg of the journey.

"Alright, Lucy," Ben said. "I have to get to bed. We're

leaving early tomorrow."

"I do too," Lucy said.

They stood and entered the elevator. The door began to shut before Lucy entered, so Ben held the door for her.

"What a gentleman," Lucy said.

Ben blushed slightly. Lucy pressed the button for the top floor, while Ben pressed the button for a few floors lower. Tense silence occupied the elevator. Ben glanced sideways at Lucy, who fiddled with her room key. Finally, the elevator door opened on Ben's floor. He took one step toward the door and hesitated.

Ben turned and stood in front of Lucy. He gazed into her eyes, into her soul. He lifted her chin lightly and kissed her. She returned the gesture.

The elevator door closed. Lucy pushed Ben against the elevator wall. Her hands rubbed across his back and his hands rubbed across hers. They kissed passionately; a physical representation of a deeper personal connection. Ben felt electrified.

The elevator moved up toward the top floor. It stopped with a jolt and the door opened. Lucy pulled herself away from Ben. They looked at each other for a second that seemed like an hour. Lucy stepped toward the door and stood in the elevator doorway.

"I'll see you in New York, Mr. Benjamin Emerson," Lucy said.

Ben just looked at her in adoration. He could not think of any clever response, so he just smiled. A true, genuine smile that came from his heart.

The elevator door closed and Ben returned to his own floor. He entered his hotel room and flopped onto his own bed. He tried to fall asleep because he knew that tomorrow's early morning wake-up would be difficult, but his mind had a singular focus. He knew his body was in his own bed, but his mind was upstairs with Lucy.

# CHAPTER 15

The Jeep surged onto the freeway and tucked between two sedans that failed to allow proper merge spacing. Each sedan blared warning signals, both verbal and auditory. Soon, the Jeep's highway intersected with another, so the Jeep was forced to merge into morning traffic once again. It merged onto its final highway connection and slugged into New York City.

The Jeep's ragtop lowered, which allowed the dense morning air to flow throughout the cockpit. The sun rose over skyscrapers as the Jeep crossed from New Jersey to New York over the Hudson River. Ben sensed the East Coast city grit emerge from the hot, asphalt streets.

Ben and Chris felt nervous about their next steps. They drove aimlessly into the City, so they began to formulate their action plan. Chris planned to negotiate for his JP Morgan Chase job, which would enable the boys to live in their apartment complex for free. If that plan failed, then Chris had no more options for success, but he felt confident that Ben's spontaneity would move their actions forward. First, they needed a parking spot, which was a nearly impossible acquisition during prime traffic hours. Chris had an idea.

The Jeep pulled into the parking garage of a condominium establishment near Thomas Paine Park. A well-groomed parking attendant requested to see Chris' apartment identification, which Chris was unable to produce. Chris portrayed himself with aura of class and distinction.

"I haven't officially checked into my new apartment," Chris said. "Can I park here while I check in? I'm with JP Morgan Chase."

"Of course, sir," the attendant said. "The Spencer is a very established living facility and we have a mutually beneficial partnership with JP Morgan Chase. Leave your car here until you get everything squared away. If you need help settling in, just ask Steve at the front desk."

Chris parked the Jeep and walked into the apartment complex lobby. He knew that his lease for the apartment at The Spencer was no longer valid, but he decided to check with the front desk, which informed him that his suspicion was correct. Chris and Ben walked out of the lobby and onto the street.

"So, we have no place to live," Chris said. "What are we going to do?"

"I don't know, man," Ben said. "What should we do with your car?"

"Let's leave it in that parking garage for the day," Chris said. "The parking guy told me we could leave it there until we got our living situation squared away. He meant at The

Spencer, but he doesn't need to know that we won't be living there at all. We'll get the car later."

The boys strolled aimlessly down the street and stopped at the crosswalk.

"So we have a few options," Chris said. "We can spend all day finding an apartment and use JP Morgan Chase's credit card to pay for our first month's rent. Or we can crash in a hotel tonight."

"What if the credit card gets declined?" Ben asked.

"It won't. If JP Morgan hasn't cancelled the card yet, I doubt they will today," Chris said. "And if it is cancelled, we can sleep on the street, which I would prefer not to do."

"Yeah, the street doesn't seem too comfortable or safe," Ben said.

"Let's get a coffee and plan our attack," Chris said.

The boys entered a corner coffee shop. Chris ordered two coffees. He handed the JP Morgan Chase credit card to the cashier, who swiped the card.

"Your card was declined, sir," the cashier said.

"Can you please try again?" Chris asked.

The cashier swiped the card again and it declined for a second time. Chris paid with the remaining cash in his wallet. As he handed his remaining cash to the cashier, he felt his last strand of pride go with it. He handed one coffee to Ben and the boys returned to the street.

"Well, we're almost out of money," Chris said. "I was banking on my Wall Street firm to float me until I earned my first paycheck. I don't have much money saved up from college because I didn't work, like you did. I could call my parents, but I don't want to. I want to show them that I can do this on my own."

"I have enough money to feed us for the day," Ben said, "but that's all. I spent more money on this trip than I thought I would."

The sun fried the concrete jungle as Chris and Ben strolled toward the Brooklyn Bridge. With each step, Chris lost hope in his grasp on life. His job title no longer existed. His potential for high social status was gone. By morning, he could be homeless; sleeping on the street in the Jeep was looking like the most plausible option for the night, unless he could negotiate for his former job title. He spent the last cash stash he owned and, since he measured his success numerically by his available cash flow, Chris felt his own self-worth deplete with every step.

Ben purchased two hot dogs and a water from a street vendor near the Bridge, which left him enough money to buy an inexpensive dinner and maybe two beers. After that, the boys' financial tank would be empty.

They boys entered the flow of foot traffic as they walked across the Brooklyn Bridge. Ben snapped photographs of the view and of the variety of people that strolled and hustled to their next destinations.

When they reached the middle of the bridge, Chris stopped. His heart quickened pace, which matched the rapid, depressed thoughts that swirled through his mind. The power of lost aspirations began to overtake Chris' common sense. He neared the railing and peered over the side at the water below his feet.

"What if I just jumped?" Chris asked.

Ben peered sideways at his friend. Worry floated in his chest.

"What do you mean?" Ben asked.

"I mean, what if I just jumped off of this bridge?" Chris said. "No one would miss me. I have no effect on this world anymore."

"Chris, stop that line of thinking," Ben said.

"Seriously, though," Chris continued, "I have no job, I have no money, I have no family except for my parents, but they don't care enough about me to notice. They're worse than Geoffrey's parents. All they care about is their damn money and social image. I could jump and let the river sweep me away and no one would think twice."

Ben turned away from the view and looked directly at Chris.

"Shut up, dude," Ben said. "Everyone would miss you. Your parents would be devastated, and I would have no one to help me through New York City."

Ben paused and allowed Chris to ponder those thoughts. Chris leaned forward and looked at the water again.

"I don't even make an impact on the world, so why should I take up space here?" Chris asked.

Chris gripped the railing. He lifted his foot and placed one shoe on the rail's edge.

"Seriously, stop that line of thinking," Ben said. "You need to stop playing the role of the victim. If you don't think that you're making an impact on the world, then go make one. It's that simple."

"But how do I make an impact on the world, Ben?" Chris shouted.

"I'm trying to figure that out for myself," Ben said.

Chris lowered his shoe. The boys stood and watched the City's ebb and flow. Or maybe it was the river that flowed. People moved behind the boys. Everyone was engaged in their own personal worlds. No one was aware that trouble brewed in the lives of these two boys.

Ben reflected on his impact on society, which was small at this point in his life; he thought about his potential for the future and he recognized that he had the ability to impact his culture greatly.

Chris continued to stare at the moving, murky water and pondered his place in life and society. He knew that he may never exceed his family's high social status, but maybe he began to accept that possibility. Finally, the heavy pressure of the situation exceeded Ben's patience.

"If you jumped, your Jeep would be pissed!" Ben shouted.

That caused Chris to smile against his will.

"You're right," Chris said. "I would hate to leave my Jeep in your hands."

Both boys laughed. Ben needed to remove Chris from his state of impending bridge depression, so he turned and walked, hoping that Chris would follow. After moving a few steps away from the ledge, Ben turned and saw Chris jogging to catch him.

"Let's go explore our new home," Ben said. "Maybe a talk with JP Morgan himself will help your situation. We have nothing to lose. I'm the richest one of us now, and that's not saying much. Let's stroll by Wall Street and see what we can do."

The boys merged into the crowd and walked to the end of the Brooklyn Bridge. Even though the day had not yet reached noon, the sun made the concrete boil. Ben perspired from his forehead. Chris felt thirsty from the heat.

Across the street, a desperate young man noticed Ben

and Chris. He could see that they were new to the Big Apple. He crossed the street and approached the boys from the right side. He walked slowly; his sneakers, basketball shorts, and oversized white t-shirt allowed him to blend with the mass of people. He merged with the sidewalk crowd and aimed to pass behind the boys.

Ben felt a hand slide into his back pocket. He grasped for his wallet, but it was gone. He whipped his head around and saw his wallet move into the young man's pocket. Ben's wallet contained the remainder of the boys' finances.

"Hey!" Ben shouted.

The man made eye contact with Ben and began to sprint through the crowd. Ben sprinted after him. The man pushed a woman to the side and dashed to the right. He ran in the middle of the street before crossing to the opposite sidewalk.

Ben followed. His adrenaline propelled him forward with desperation. Chris followed closely behind, but his unawareness of the situation forced him to move slower than Ben.

The pickpocket juked into an alleyway. Ben juked faster. He reached his hand out to grab the man's shirt, but his hip hit a garbage can and slowed his acceleration. The pickpocket looked over his shoulder and Ben caught a clear image of his face; the image seemed to freeze in time, almost like a photograph.

The pickpocket had a small tattoo on his neck. His brown eyes looked alert and full of life, unlike a man who was addicted to a toxic substance, though his kind eyes exuded desperation. He was young, maybe three years younger than Ben. Light fluttered into the alleyway and Ben saw the man's dark, African skin, topped with an unkempt afro. Momentarily, Ben questioned the seemingly kind-hearted man's motives for his pickpocket actions.

Ben shouted at the man, which caused him to break into a full sprint. He exited the alleyway and cut onto the sidewalk. Ben followed. He was thankful for his usual morning exercise routine, as he was gaining ground on the pickpocket, whose stamina was fading. Ben sweated profusely. His shirt began to fill with moisture.

The pickpocket hopped over an old fence into the Trinity Church graveyard and he hid behind Alexander Hamilton's grave. Ben saw him jump over the fence, but he lost the pickpocket as he hid.

In 1804, Alexander Hamilton was killed by Vice President Aaron Burr in a duel over honor. Now, Ben felt the need to defend his honor and pride at the expense of the pickpocket. He felt a rage boil in his gut; an anger he had felt only once, an anger that cultivates only from desperation.

Ben sprung over the graveyard fence and dashed between headstones. He saw the pickpocket crouching. The pickpocket spun and exited the graveyard through an open gate. Ben ran at an angle and jumped over the fence.

The pickpocket crossed the street and paused on the corner of Wall Street and Broadway. He swiveled his head around to look for Ben. When he found the victim, Ben was running at full speed toward him.

Ben did not stop. He dropped his shoulder and tackled the pickpocket with full force. Ben's wallet flew from the man's pocket. Chris finally caught up with the chase and retrieved the wallet from the ground. Ben lifted the young pickpocket by his shirt and shouted in his face.

"I'll kill you!" Ben shouted.

"I'm sorry!" the pickpocket stuttered.

"You're sorry?" Ben shouted. "You stole the only money I have left!"

"I'm sorry, man!" the pickpocket stuttered again.

A crowd gathered around the scuffle. Chris began to feel pressure to act; Ben saw only the pickpocket through tunnel-vision lenses.

"I'm going to kill him, Chris," Ben said.

Chris looked at the pickpocket and saw a familiar situation; a reflection stared back at him. A new sense of empathy overcame him. Chris stepped to Ben with a calm demeanor.

"Let him go, Ben" Chris said. "He's desperate, just like us."

"I'm only 21 years old, man," the pickpocket said. "Both of my parents are dead and I have no money and no way to get it. I don't have a home, man. I just need to eat. I really am desperate. I had no choice, man. I don't want to go to jail, man. Please don't call the cops."

Ben released the man's shirt and took three steps in reverse. As his adrenaline subsided, he began to shake. Ben's thoughts cleared and he became aware of the crowd that surrounded the scene.

He reflected on his actions and his words toward the pickpocket and he felt immediate regret for allowing rage to override his moral code.

"I'm sorry, man," Ben said. "We're desperate too."

He extended his hand toward the pickpocket in an act of forgiveness, an action which the pickpocket reciprocated.

The crowd, hoping to witness a fight, dispersed when it became evident that violence was absent from the scene. The mob did not want to witness forgiveness.

Chris looked around at the intersection of Wall Street and Broadway. He gazed down Wall Street and saw the New York Stock Exchange building, an enterprise that he admired whole-heartedly until his drive with Ben. Chris looked further down the street and saw the offices of JP Morgan Chase, another enterprise that he used to adore. Now, his feelings of admiration toward the financial giant wore thin. Ben's attitude toward money as a driving force for happiness seeped into Chris' moral fibers.

Two elite men dressed in expensive suits exited the JP Morgan Chase building and strolled purposefully in the boys' direction on the corner of Wall Street and Broadway. Chris recognized one of the suited men as the Chase employee who hired him for the entry-level finance position.

He recognized the other man as Stephen O'Connell, the Chase employee who called him to let him go. The suited men passed the pickpocket and Ben, but Chris stepped toward them.

"Mr. O'Connell," Chris said.

Stephen O'Connell looked at Chris with distained unfamiliarity.

"I'm Christopher Morgan," Chris said. "You two hired me for a financial analyst position a few months ago, but my position was cut."

Mr. O'Connell looked at the other suited man. They both smirked with egotistical recognition.

"Hello, Mr. Morgan," Mr. O'Connell said. "What brings

you to New York?"

"I was on my way to work for you when you called to fire me," Chris said.

Mr. O'Connell frowned with false empathy.

"Well, I'm sorry about that, Mr. Morgan," Mr. O'Connell said. "I hope you're enjoying the City. We'll see you around."

The two businessmen hustled away from the encounter with no remorse for Chris' situation. Immediately, they renewed their discussions about their personal business gains.

Ben heard the entire discussion between Chris and the JP Morgan Chase executives. He felt complete empathy for Chris, who now cowered in defeat. Ben looked at Chris with strength. He nodded his head in the direction of the businessmen. The nod gave Chris a sense of purpose. Chris followed Ben's nod and jogged after the executives.

"Hey!" Chris shouted.

Mr. O'Connell and his associate turned. They looked at Chris: a poor, sweaty, disheveled young man who projected justice in his glare. They lifted their noses in perceived superiority based on their social status.

"You really screwed me over. You know that, right?" Chris said.

"That's business," Mr. O'Connell said. "We have to do what's in the best interest of our company."

"But that's not what you did," Chris said. "You did what was in the best interest for you and your damn wallets."

"Excuse me, young man, but you don't have the right to speak to me that way," Mr. O'Connell said. "Do you know who I am? I'm one of the richest people in New York City."

"I know exactly who you are," Chris said. "You're a self-absorbed money-taker who has no interest in the betterment of his company, only in the fattening of his own wallet. You base your happiness on your social status and the numbers in your bank accounts. The only self-worth you possess is your money and your power."

Chris' ferocity flared through his tone and through his powerful stance.

"But I know who you really are. Take away the money and you lose your status. Take away your money, and you lose your influence. Nobody respects you for your character. Nobody respects you for your sense of adventure, or your humor, or your tolerance of others. You hide behind your mask of wealth because you're scared to let anybody see who you've become: a heartless tyrant who steals money from his employees and customers through inflated commission costs for the purpose of paying for another high-rise condo in The Hamptons just so people will think more highly of you. When, in fact, your wife and kids probably left you because you're a dick. Money rotted your soul and ripped out your heart."

Chris paused to breathe.

"And, to think, I wanted to be just like you," Chris said.

Mr. O'Connell's eyes grew wider with every word. His business partner looked at Chris with admiration, yet he still recoiled with each verbal blow. Mr. O'Connell felt completely defeated by the verbal tirade from a member of low social status. Even people in his own social class did not speak to him with such firepower. Mr. O'Connell's thoughts were clouded by pride.

"Mr. Morgan," Mr. O'Connell said," with that kind of

passion, you would make an incredible financial analyst. I would like to offer you a higher paying job within our company. With that kind of attitude, I would like you to be my understudy. I'll teach you what it takes to reach the top, and then to keep reaching."

Chris felt victory in his soul. Mr. O'Connell just offered him the job of his dreams.

Chris began to speak, but then stopped and thought. This was not the job of his dreams; this was the dream job of his former self, the dream of job of the rich kid from Boston, the dream job of the ambitious-yet-misguided Chris who had not experienced the complete culture of Americana. Chris wanted more than riches and power. He was more ambitious than that.

"With all due respect, Mr. O'Connell," Chris said, "I'm going to have to decline your offer. I'm better than that."

Mr. O'Connell's face expressed shock. His business partner looked at Chris with stupefied bewilderment. Mr. O'Connell's pride was bruised again.

"No one turns down a job at JP Morgan Chase," Mr. O'Connell said.

"Well, I just did," Chris said. "I hope you're enjoying the City. I'll see you around."

Chris turned and walked toward Ben and the pickpocket. The JP Morgan Chase executives stood frozen on the corner of Wall Street and Broadway.

# CHAPTER 16

Chris looked at Ben with an expression of pride and self-doubt mixed with analytical reflection.

"Am I an idiot for turning down a better job at JP Morgan Chase?" Chris asked.

"No way. You're a genius!" Ben said. "You stood up to the richest, most corrupt guys in New York City and battled them with values instead of money. They didn't know what to do. It was great."

Chris, Ben, and Pickpocket stood on the corner of Wall Street and Broadway and watched the defeated financial executives disappear into the crowd. Pickpocket stood paradoxically; he felt like he should escape since he had tried to rob Ben, but he felt compelled to stay. Chris' virtuous stand against financial injustice empowered Pickpocket, while Ben's forgiveness gave him hope.

"Guys," Pickpocket said, "I'm really sorry I stole your wallet. I'm desperate and I don't know what else to do. But I want to be more honest. That right there, that inspired me to be better."

He looked at Chris and nodded to emphasize his earnestness. Then he looked at Ben.

"And the fact that you forgave a thief like me, man, that changed me," Pickpocket continued. "I mean, you caught me. I should be face-down on the pavement getting arrested right now, but instead, I'm looking at a second chance. An opportunity to follow the right path. I'm on some Robert Frost shit."

Ben nodded his head toward Pickpocket, who reciprocated the gesture.

"I'm a good person, I swear. I just need to eat, you know?" Pickpocket said.

"We understand, man," Ben said. "At this point, we're in the same situation. We don't have jobs. We don't have a place to live. And we barely have enough money to eat today."

"Well, what are you going to do about it?" Pickpocket asked.

"I don't know," Ben said. "I really don't. What are you going to do?"

"I don't know, man," Pickpocket said. "But I'm going to be better. And I can thank you guys for that. You showed me forgiveness when anybody else would have shown me revenge. I owe it to you to be better."

"You owe it to yourself, man," Ben said. "You're a good kid. Do something with those values."

"I will," Pickpocket said. "I'll see you guys around."

Pickpocket turned and disappeared into the crowd. Ben and Chris decided that they were hungry and that they would find a place to eat their last meal using their last dollars. A clock tower showed *3:00 p.m.*, which meant the boys would eat a late lunch or early dinner.

Chris and Ben strolled up Broadway. They passed theatres and expensive restaurants. They passed well-dressed business people and grungy people who had no home. Chris and Ben fit somewhere in between the New York City income gap. After their last meal, they would fall to the bottom of the financial totem pole, but they continued to rise to the top of the City's most virtuous individuals with every just action and renunciation of wealth as an idol.

The boys walked for an hour for two reasons: to reach a less expensive part of town and to extend their hunger into dinner time. Finally, they reached New York University and decided that they needed to eat. They turned on a side street and found a small Irish pub called McSorley's Old Ale House. According to the bar sign, McSorley's had been in business since 1854, making it the oldest Irish pub in the City.

Darkness enveloped the boys' vision when they entered McSorley's. When their eyes adjusted, they saw that the pub remained physically unchanged since its opening in 1854. Dark wood covered the entire establishment. The floorboards were uneven and the wood beam columns were not entirely level. Sawdust covered the floor, which kept the street dirt from tarnishing the hardwood. The walls were covered in photographs and New York City memorabilia.

One man sat on a rickety bar stool, while a few other small groups sat at tables in the narrow bar room. Ben and Chris sat at a two-person table near two old men. A server approached the boys' table and asked for their order. In his thick Irish accent, the server informed the boys that the bar served beer in half pint glasses and that they only had two beer options: light and dark. Ben ordered two half pints of dark beer, while Chris ordered two half pints of light beer. They each ordered a sandwich. Since the half pints were so cheap, Ben calculated that the boys could order another round of half pints after they finished their dinner.

Chris stood to use the restroom, which left Ben alone at the table. He felt an urge to write. He needed to voice his frustrations from his current life situation. For the first time in his life, he truly feared the impending uncertainty that awaited him. Ben opened his journal and began to write:

*July 5, 2015*

*This might be my last journal entry ever. At this point, I'm stranded in the world's biggest concrete jungle with no home, no food, and no money. I've squeezed out of some tricky situations during this adventure, but this one seems insurmountable. I'll have to sleep on the street tonight, I'm sure, because the car probably got towed. If I make it through til morning, all my effort will focus on obtaining money by any means necessary, as Malcolm X said.*

*I just spent my last dollar on a mug of dark beer from this Irish bar. Where we'll go from this wooden bench, I can't say, but it won't be an easy journey any more. It's been a fun ride while it lasted. I'm out.*

*Ben E.*

Chris returned from the restroom. As he strolled toward their seats, Ben noticed that Chris was exploring the various historical artifacts that surrounded the barroom walls. Eventually, Chris made it to his seat.

"Are you writing again?" Chris asked. "Stupid question. You're always writing."

"It helps me gather my thoughts," Ben said.

"What are you writing about?" Chris asked.

"How terrified I am of the future," Ben said.

The old men seated next to the boys heard Ben's voice and noticed a Pacific Northwest accent, so one man leaned into the boys' table. His white moustache and old Yankees cap insinuated his deep New York roots.

"Where are you boys from?" the old man asked in a thick, quivering New York accent.

"I'm from Oregon," Ben said.

"Far away from here," the old man said. "What brings you to a place like McSorley's?"

"We were looking for a bar, and this is what we found," Ben said.

"Well, it's a good place to land," the old man said. "I grew up down the street and I went to New York University down the way and now I live above the bar. I've been going to McSorley's for 60 years."

"That's amazing," Ben said. "I'll bet you've seen some cool stuff."

"You bet I have," the old man said. "Jimmy and I were here during the Blackout in 1977. People were looting buildings all over the city, but not here. Not at McSorley's. We all got free drinks!"

"Free drinks are wonderful," Ben said.

"You know," the old man continued, "women weren't allowed into this pub until 1970. I was here in this very chair on the day that a woman first walked into the bar. Boy, were we mean to her. Men were shouting and spitting and pouring drinks on that poor lady. I was part of it, I'll tell you that. Looking back on that day, I'll never forgive myself for acting like a misogynistic pig, but it was something historic to be a part of."

Ben sat back in his chair and absorbed this opportunity to listen to a primary source of New York City history. The two old men felt a sense of pride in telling their story to two young men. In a way, the old men saw parts of themselves and their own history in Ben and Chris.

"You should stand up and take a look around the walls," the old man said. "There's plenty of history in this old place."

The old man returned to the solace of his own table and to the companionship of his old friend.

With a mug of dark beer in his hand, Ben stood and began to roam around the bar. On the wall, he found a framed, oversized ticket to the opening ceremony of the Brooklyn Bridge from 1883, which gave Ben a sense of appreciation for his earlier crossing of the historic overpass. He found the Greek letters of his own college fraternity, which evoked a sentiment of reflection upon his triumphant days at University of Oregon. Ben noticed handcuffs connected to the bar railing. The bartender informed him that they belonged to Harry Houdini, the famed escape artist that grew to legendary status. The bartender told Ben that U.S. Presidents, like Abraham Lincoln, Ulysses S. Grant, and Theodore Roosevelt visited the bar, while one of Ben's favorite writers, Hunter S. Thompson, was a regular McSorley's patron. This gave Ben a feeling of insignificance in history, yet he felt as if he stood in a time capsule of incredible memories, thoughts, and revolutions.

Then, Ben noticed dusty wishbones on a ledge behind the bar. The bartender said that the wishbones were left there by soldiers before they deployed to Europe during World War One. The remaining wishbones were from the soldiers who did not return from the battlefield.

Ben thought of his own father and the fact that he did not return home. To Ben, one of those wishbones represented his father. Tears began to well in his eyes. Ben reflected on his father's place in history in comparison to the soldiers that these wishbones represented. Then, Ben thought of his own small place in history in comparison to the people that these historical relics represented. *How will I make my mark on history?* Ben wondered.

Ben returned to his seat. His face expressed deep concentration and slight concern. Chris noticed his facial tone immediately.

"What's wrong, Ben?" Chris asked.

"Nothing is wrong," Ben said. "I just don't want to be insignificant, you know? I don't want my life to be wasted. I want to make an impact on the world in some way. Even if it's a small impact, I want to leave the world a better place than it was before I got here."

"You will, Ben," Chris said. "You and I, we have the opportunity to be great."

Ben took a bite of his sandwich and washed it down with a gulp of dark beer.

"How can we be great?" Ben asked. "I know we can be, but how do we do it?"

"I don't know," Chris said. "Before this road trip, I

thought I knew how to be great, but now, I'm not sure what the right course of action is."

Ben thought for a moment and took another sandwich bite.

"Chris, what makes you happy?" Ben asked,

"Working with money, I suppose," Chris said. "But I just turned down the opportunity to work with more money than I can even fathom."

"That job also came with the baggage of acquiring more money than you'd know what to do with," Ben said. "And the burden of stealing money from other people."

"You're right," Chris said. "So how do I proceed?"

"Find a way to pursue working *with* money, not *obtaining* money for yourself," Ben said. "Find a way to make a lot of money through a virtuous cause instead of personal benefit."

"Making money for a noble purpose, huh," Chris said. "Maybe I can find a non-profit organization that can use my financial skillset."

Ben raised his second half pint of dark beer and Chris connected with his second half pint of light beer. The glass mugs crashed together. The two old men looked at the boys and smiled as they reminisced over their countless cheers in McSorley's.

"What about you, Benny?" Chris asked. "What makes you happy?"

"All kinds of things," Ben said. "Mostly writing and taking photos, I suppose."

"Why does writing make you happy?" Chris asked.

"Writing is an avenue to express my ideas and to allow people to see the world through my perspective," Ben said.

"I like to write because there's never a perfect piece of writing, but I like to pursue perfection. I find happiness in the pursuit more that the final product. Piecing together a perfectly composed story or poem is challenging and fun because I know that no matter how much effort I put into the piece, there will always be flaws, just like in life. No matter how hard I try to be a perfect person, I will always be flawed."

"And photography?" Chris asked.

"It's similar to writing," Ben said. "If I can capture life's moments in one still frame that reflects the way I see that moment, I consider that a successful photograph, but it's impossible to capture a moment exactly as I see it; therefore, there's never a perfect photograph. No matter how many angles I shoot from, no matter how much I alter the aperture and shutter speed, I can never reflect my vision of the world perfectly, but I enjoy the pursuit because I get closer to perfection every time I try, even through my failures."

Chris took a drink of his light beer and nodded his head in acceptance of Ben's responses.

"So," Chris said, "use that passion and your skills to make the world better. Write stories that make the people understand the world's issues through your eyes. Take photographs that showcase the ups and downs of daily life. Become a writer and a photographer. Cement your place in history by expressing your ideas through those avenues."

Ben smiled. Both boys raised their glasses. This time, the old men did, too.

# CHAPTER 17

Ben and Chris walked out of the darkness of McSorley's Old Ale House and stepped into the bright evening air that enveloped the New York University area.

Ben felt a vibration come from his pocket. His reflexes caused him to clamp his hand down on his hip; the memory of the pickpocket still loomed. Then, he realized that his phone was ringing. He picked it up without glancing to see who was calling.

"Hello?" Chris said.

"Hey, Benny. It's Samantha."

Ben's heart dropped.

"What's up, Sam?" Ben said.

Chris looked at Ben with a shocked expression. He motioned for Ben to hang up the phone.

"I just wanted to let you know that I'm leaving for Miami tomorrow," Samantha said. "I want you to come over to my apartment for dinner tonight. Maybe we can spend one last night with each other before I leave."

Ben grew angry at the proposition.

"Sam," Ben said, "I moved to New York City. In fact, I'm here right now."

"You moved to New York?" Samantha said. "I thought you would wait for me to return to Portland someday."

"That's ridiculous, Sam," Ben said.

"But, Benny," Samantha started, "why would you move to New York? You won't be able to do…"

Ben interrupted her.

"I've come to a realization. Even if I were still in the Northwest, I wouldn't come over tonight. I need someone who respects me and who cares about the world over herself."

Samantha was silent from the other end of the phone.

Chris looked across the street and saw a familiar blonde-and-brunette duo cross toward the boys. He punched Chris in the shoulder and directed his attention to Lucy, who approached them.

"In fact, Sam," Ben said, "I have found that person. Adios."

Ben hung up the phone and shoved it in his pocket. Lucy sprinted toward Ben and he hugged her tightly. He felt like crying from emotion overload, but instead, he kissed Lucy.

"I can't believe we ran into you again!" Mary Anne shouted over the New York City noise.

"What are you guys doing?" Lucy asked.

"We don't really know," Ben said.

"We're heading to Mary Anne's brother apartment, but we should meet up later tonight, or tomorrow," Lucy said. "I know you guys are moving in today, right?"

"Well, not exactly," Chris said. "We don't have a spot to

live anymore, so we need to figure that out before the day is over."

Lucy looked at Mary Anne empathetically.

"If you need a place to stay for a couple days, I'm sure you could stay with us at my brother's apartment," Mary Anne said.

"Thank you so much," Ben said. "Maybe we'll take you up on that offer."

"Alright, ladies," Chris said. "We need to get a move on, but we'll definitely call you later on."

Ben hugged Lucy again. The boys continued on their path and the girls moved in their own direction.

Chris needed to find his Jeep before sunset so the boys would have a place to sleep. With an hour's walk ahead of them, Ben and Chris strolled briskly down Broadway toward Wall Street. Though sunset was a few hours away, New York City's skyscrapers hid the setting sun from view and created a neon twilight effect. As the boys passed a small Broadway theatre, the effect grew stronger.

A door to the theatre opened and a middle-aged women emerged. She carried an oversized canvas beach bag and wore baggy clothing; she looked like a model for Bohemian style. As she searched her bag for her glasses, she walked toward the boys with her head facing the sidewalk. Ben turned to talk to Chris. The woman bumped into Ben and she dropped her glasses. Ben reached down and grabbed the glasses and handed them to the woman. She placed the glasses on her face and looked at Ben. Her face brightened; Ben's eyes widened.

"Benny!" the woman shouted.

She threw her arms around his neck and hugged him

tightly.

"Mom?" Ben shouted.

Chris stood back in bewilderment at the coincidence.

"Mom," Ben said, "what are you doing here?"

"I just finished an audition for a play," Mrs. Emerson said.

"Which play?" Ben asked.

"*Fiddler on the Roof*," Mrs. Emerson said. "I auditioned for the part of Yente the Matchmaker. It's just a small production. Nothing major, like something you'd see at a big theatre."

Ben's mother smiled sheepishly, which revealed a lack of confidence in her audition performance.

"What are you doing here, Benny?" Mrs. Emerson asked.

"At this point, I don't really know," Ben said.

He smiled sheepishly like his mother; a smile that returned him to a boyhood state.

"I thought you were living in Portland and starting your job with that big public relations company," Mrs. Emerson said.

"I'm learning that life doesn't always follow a road map," Ben said.

Ben introduced his mother to Chris, who shook hands professionally and politely. Ben's mother looked at the boys with adoration and protective instinct.

Chris explained the boys' situation: that Chris encouraged Ben to move to New York City with him, that they travelled through biker-gang-infested Sturgis, passed by Mount Rushmore, rolled with the elite patrons of Minnesota, argued with the powers of West Virginia, and drank in the Philadelphia shadows of the Founding Fathers on their way to New York City, where a job that never even existed awaited them.

"I'm so sorry that you're both down on your luck," Mrs. Emerson said. "But I wouldn't say that you're down and out. It sounds to me like you boys had yourself an incredible adventure."

Ben and Chris looked at each other and laughed.

"Yes we did, ma'am," Chris said.

"Come on, boys," Mrs. Emerson said. "My apartment isn't too far from here. You can stay with me until you find your place."

"Thanks, Mom," Ben said.

"Yes, thank you so much," Chris said. "I have my Jeep parked nearby. Is there a place by your apartment building that I can leave it?"

"I have a parking space that comes with my apartment, but I don't have a car, so I never use it," Mrs. Emerson said. "I'm lucky. No one gets a parking spot in New York."

"So you got your luck from your mom, Benny?" Chris said.

Chris left to retrieve his Jeep, which left Ben alone with his mother as they walked toward her apartment building. With Chris gone, Ben felt awkward. He had not spoken face-to-face with his mother in years. He felt abandoned. Part of him wanted to lash out against her for leaving him alone in the Pacific Northwest. Another part of him yearned to forgive her and understand her perspective. Their short walk consisted of surface-level discussion and long, silent pauses.

The Jeep turned the corner and parked in a parking garage near Mrs. Emerson's apartment building just as Ben and his mother arrived. Chris emerged from the garage staircase and found Ben, who was waiting to unload their gear.

Ben flung his backpack over his shoulder. He checked the floor to make sure he had retrieved all of his belongings. Chris opened the glove box to ensure that no valuables were left in the ragtop overnight.

As soon as he opened the compartment latch, his eyes widened. He gasped audibly. He pulled an envelope from the compartment and dashed toward Ben to show him the contents.

"We have 2,500 dollars, Ben!" Chris said. "How did we forget about this?"

Ben's heart raced. He shook with excitement.

"We're rich!" Ben shouted. "But what should we do with it?"

"It's not ours, and its dirty money," Chris said. "This money was a bribe for my uncle from those damn bootleggers."

Chris hesitated, but the apprehension of leaving an envelope full of cash in the palm of his hand in broad daylight in the middle of the City forced him to act eventually. He placed the envelope awkwardly in his front pocket.

"Let's just keep it in our pocket until we think of something," Chris said.

Chris took a trunk and a bag to the apartment while Ben waited on the street with the remainder of the luggage. Chris returned shortly. He breathed heavily from the lengthy staircase descent.

Ben looked around at the twilight City. The foot traffic

seemed thin compared to earlier that morning. Ben's gaze shifted across the street; he saw a familiar figure strolling on the sidewalk across from the apartment complex. The man's body language suggested depression and desperation with a good-natured conscience.

"Hey, Pickpocket!" Ben shouted.

The man turned his head, revealing kind eyes. He recognized Ben and Chris, so he ran across the street to them.

"I told you that I'd see you boys around," Pickpocket said.

He smiled widely and shook hands with Ben and Chris.

"You weren't kidding," Chris said.

"So, is this where you guys live?" Pickpocket asked.

"It's where my mom lives, so I guess we live here for now," Ben said.

"Where do you live?" Chris asked.

"In a homeless shelter down the street, as long as they have a bed available for me," Pickpocket said.

Ben looked at Chris and saw his eyes brighten with an idea. Chris reached into his pocket and removed the envelope with 2,500 dollars and handed it to Pickpocket.

"Maybe this will give you the jumpstart you need," Chris said.

Pickpocket opened the envelope and his eyes lit up. He smiled wide and hugged Chris and expressed his gratitude. He put the envelope in his pocket. Chris half-expected Pickpocket to run, but he remained with the boys.

"Hey, Pickpocket," Chris said, "who runs the shelter where you sleep?"

"It's a new organization," Pickpocket said. "I think it's

religiously based, not controlled by some government organization. It's a non-profit group called *Hand Up*. They're good people. They really do make a difference."

"Do you think they have any job openings?" Chris asked.

"I'm sure this group could use all the help they can find," Pickpocket said.

"So you're saying they could use a *hand up*?" Ben said. He paused and waited for the laugh.

"That was really corny, man," Pickpocket said.

They all laughed.

"Want me to take you to the shelter and introduce you to the woman who runs the place?" Pickpocket asked Chris.

"That would be amazing," Chris said.

"Cool. It's only about five blocks away," Pickpocket said.

The sun set below the horizon, but the city lights fired through the twilight sky. Chris and Pickpocket walked to the homeless shelter. Ben unloaded the car and his mother helped him bring the bags and trunks up to her apartment on the fourteenth level.

Ben walked into the apartment and noticed that it was not much larger than his own college fraternity room, although his mother's residence had a small deck with a coffee table and two chairs, an addition which pleased Ben. In the main room, a floral-patterned sofa sat in front of a small television. A kitchenette branched into a semi-separate room, which left enough space for an oven and a miniature refrigerator. Mrs. Emerson led her son to the extra bedroom, which did not have a bed. Ben and Chris would have to sleep on the floor, but Ben figured that it was better than sleeping in the Jeep's front seat.

"Can I make you some tea, Benny?" Mrs. Emerson said,

walking into the living room.

"That would be great, Mom," Ben said.

He felt awkward, yet childlike. His mother rarely waited on him, especially after Ben's father died.

Ben opened the sliding door to the deck and sat at the coffee table. From the deck, he overlooked an alleyway. If he strained his head a bit, he could see the street to his left. The alleyway had substantial foot traffic, especially for late in the evening. Ben's mother emerged from the kitchen with two mugs of green tea. Even in the summer heat, Ben saw the steam rise from the liquid. Ben's mother sat in the other chair on the deck.

"Ben, how long have you been in the City?" Mrs. Emerson asked.

"We pulled in this morning," Ben said.

"Why didn't you tell me that you decided to move to New York?" Mrs. Emerson said.

Ben hesitated. He knew this question would surface eventually. He felt awkward about calling his mother. They had spent so much time apart that their relationship seemed to fade from Ben's perspective. Since she did not fly to Oregon for Ben's college graduation, he assumed that she had vanished from his life, or that she no longer cared about her son.

"Well, Mom," Ben said, "I meant to call you, but I figured that, since you didn't come to graduation, that maybe you were busy, or that you didn't want to see me. I didn't want to be a burden."

"Benny," Mrs. Emerson said with affection, "you're my son. I love you. You know I would have flown anywhere for your graduation if I had the money to do it. To tell you the truth, I haven't found an acting job in six months. My finances are a little slim right now. I'm waitressing five nights a week just to pay for rent and the little food that I have. You know, they call New York City the *Big Apple*, but I can barely afford a darn potato."

"Yeah, I know you couldn't make it," Ben said. "I should have called. I'm sorry."

"And I'm sorry I wasn't there for your big day, sweetie," Mrs. Emerson said. "I know that I've missed out on a lot over the past four years."

"It's alright, Mom," Ben said. "And I didn't tell you that I wasn't going to work for Portland Public Relations because I wanted you to think that I had made something of myself. I know that you and Dad didn't have a lot of money, and I wanted to be the one that succeeded and got us out of poverty."

"You know, Benny, you don't have to have a lot of money to be happy and to live a successful life," Mrs. Emerson said.

Ben laughed. His mother preached the same philosophy to him that he had preached to Chris throughout the entire road trip. Ben laughed at the irony of his own worries about money and how it equated to happiness.

"I know, Mom," Ben said. "I realize that. I just want to do something that will make me happy."

"You'll find something, Benny," Mrs. Emerson said. "Acting makes me happy. I haven't found financial success with it, but I consider the pursuit of acquiring these acting roles a success. Pouring my soul into each role allows me to tell a story to the audience and it allows me to learn about other people by putting myself into their shoes. You'll find something like that, even if it doesn't make you rich."

"I understand," Ben said. "I don't really care about money. I just want to contribute to the world."

"You will, Benny," Mrs. Emerson said. "You will."

Mrs. Emerson stood and kissed her son on the forehead. She gave him a look that expressed unconditional love. She turned and left him alone on the deck.

Ben retrieved his journal and his favorite pen from his backpack. A neon sign flickered on at the edge of the alleyway and illuminated the deck with a green hue. Ben opened his journal and began to write. He had no intention of breaking his usual journal-writing style; it happened on a subconscious level. He began to write a script.

*Act I, Scene I*

*JASON wakes up in bed on the day of his college graduation…*

# EPILOGUE

Chris felt slightly burdened by the amount of number-crunching he had to accomplish, especially before tax season approached. He looked at his computer screen and rubbed his eyes; his focus had remained on the screen for the entire work day.

Now that the sun was down, he knew that he needed to leave the office. Besides, he would be late for the formal event if he did not leave soon.

He took one last look at the spreadsheet and concluded that his financial calculations could wait. Even though he was tired, he still enjoyed working with this money.

Chris stood and reached into the small closet. He retrieved his winter coat and put it on. After he flipped off the light switch, he navigated his way to the front door of his ground-level office. He shut the door behind him.

As he shut the door, a gold glimmer caught his eye. The golden sign was a relatively new addition to the door; it still gave Chris a sense of pride every time he saw it. He took two steps back so he could read the entirety of his new title: *Director of Fundraising.*

The main lobby of the office was empty aside from the front desk, where the director of the Hand Up homeless shelter's organization sat. She hung up the phone as Chris entered the room.

"Well, Chris, we did it," the Director said.

"What did we do?" Chris asked.

"Let me rephrase that," the Director said. "You did it."

"What did I do?" Chris asked.

The Director smiled.

"That was an executive from JP Morgan Chase on the telephone," the Director said. "They responded to your call, Chris. They're donating 200,000 dollars to *Hand Up*. That's the largest donation we've ever had. Finally, that'll give us enough money to lease the second level of this building and turn it into a job training facility for our homeless residents. And it's all because of *you*, Chris. You've raised over one million dollars for our organization in your first six months with us. Think about what you can do in a year. You're a financial wizard, Christopher Morgan!"

"That's amazing!" Chris shouted. "I'm so glad you picked up that phone call. I can't believe JP Morgan Chase decided to donate. I guess my conversation with Mr. O'Connell made an impact. I mean, thank you so much for giving me this opportunity. I love this place."

"It was a blessing when you walked through that door," the Director said. "We needed someone with a kind heart and a financial mind and you came to us."

"Well, Pickpocket brought me to you," Chris said.

"Well, Francis is a good kid," the Director said. "I'm glad

he was able to get back on his feet. He stopped by the other day to let me know that he rose to the supervisor position of the doughnut shop on Ninth Avenue."

Chris looked at his watch and made a move toward the front door of the homeless shelter.

"Speaking of Francis, I have to go," Chris said. "I'm meeting him down the street and we're headed to the premier."

"Oh, I'm sorry I kept you waiting, hun," the Director said. "You two have fun and tell your wonderful friend that I said congratulations."

"I'll see you on Monday, Norma," Chris said.

Chris walked out of the homeless shelter and onto the sidewalk. Light snow fell on the dark evening air, so Chris wrapped his scarf around his neck to shield himself from the chill.

As he walked, Chris passed a newspaper and magazine stand. The bundled owner was beginning to close his stand for the evening. Chris noticed January's edition of *National Geographic* magazine at the front of the kiosk. The title read: *Photographs of Americana, Part I*. Chris picked up the magazine and looked at a stunning photograph of an old, deteriorating barn. The caption informed him that the barn sat in a corn field in Iowa. Chris smiled as he looked at the photographer's name: *Benjamin Emerson*.

His eyes travelled up one shelf to The New York Times. The front page heading read: *West Virginia Governor Candidate Indicted for Money Laundering and Bribery*. Chris picked up the newspaper and read the tagline, which mentioned the multiple charges against his uncle, Joseph Morgan. Chris laughed to himself.

"I'll take the *National Geographic* and *The New York Times*, please, sir," Chris said to the kiosk owner.

"Why do you want the *Times* from this morning?" the kiosk owner asked. "This January 15th edition will be old news in a few hours."

Chris smiled knowingly and handed some cash to the kiosk owner and thanked him. He placed the magazine and the newspaper in his briefcase and quickened his pace to make up for lost time.

Chris walked a few blocks, thrust open a wooden door and stepped into McSorley's, where he found Pickpocket seated alone at a four-person table.

"What's up, Francis?" Chris said.

"Since when do you call me Francis?" Pickpocket asked.

"Sorry, Norma from *Hand Up* got me into that habit," Chris said. "This is the first time I've seen you in a tie. It's a good look for you."

He shook Pickpocket's hand.

"Man, I've been here for a half hour and our dates haven't shown up yet," Pickpocket said. "What if we get stood up?"

"Don't worry," Chris said. "I'm sure they'll be here any minute. Who is my date, anyway? You haven't told me much about her."

"Christina," Pickpocket said. "Her name is Christina. She's my cousin. She's very nice."

"You set me up on a blind date with your cousin?" Chris said.

"Of course," Pickpocket said. "You're a good guy."

Chris smiled.

"And besides," Pickpocket continued, "I'm taking her

best friend out tonight, so it works out well."

"You're always motivated, my man," Chris said.

The girls walked through the door and the gentlemen stood to greet them. Pickpocket ordered a round of light beers for the table. After surface conversations were finished and the half pint beer mugs were empty, the group left McSorley's Old Ale House and jumped in a taxi, which dropped them off on Broadway.

Chris pulled four tickets from his coat pocket and handed them to the group. Pickpocket held the door for his date, who responded with an appreciative smile.

When he entered the theatre lobby, Chris grabbed a program for the show. The group maneuvered into their seats: fifth row, center stage.

"You must have paid a fortune for these tickets," Christina said to Chris.

He chuckled politely, which appeared to be an act of modesty, but Chris laughed because he knew that the tickets were free.

Chris looked at the playbill and felt a surge of pride when he read the play's title: *American Jeep - Written By: Benjamin Emerson.* He opened the program and found the cast list. He smiled when he saw that the leading female role belonged to Ben's mother.

From the dark recesses of his backstage seat, Ben peered out at the crowded audience. He shook with nervous energy as the crowd grew. The anticipation of opening night was nearly too much for Ben, but he tried to calm himself and remain in his seat.

He saw Chris and Pickpocket take their seats near the stage. Lucy sat next to them. The stage lights reflected off of her blonde hair and made her glow.

Ben reached for his Saint Christopher and Saint Francis medals that hung from his neck. A sudden calm overcame his demeanor. The lights dimmed, the curtains opened, and the audience applauded.

# ACKNOWLEDGMENTS

First and foremost, I want to thank my wife. You're my rock and you encouraged me to finish this story when I sat for hours with writer's block. You encouraged me to publish this story even when I thought it was impossible. You read my rough drafts and provided honest feedback. And you continue to inspire me to keep my aspirations high.

I want to thank my friends for their willingness to experience ridiculous adventures with me. Our adventures together across the United States and throughout the world provide me with ideas and experiences necessary to fuel a writer's imagination. Let's keep exploring.

Of course, I want to thank my parents for instilling within me a love for writing, a capacity for adventure, and a desire to explore and understand the world. Thank you for providing me with opportunities to grow and for helping me when I faltered and, of course, for loving me unconditionally.

# ABOUT THE AUTHOR

Tom Malone was born and raised in Portland, Oregon. He studied journalism and history at the University of Oregon, Spanish at *la Universidad de Oviedo*, and earned his master's degree in teaching from the University of Portland.

He has taken dozens of road trips throughout the United States and continues to travel throughout the world. Currently, Malone teaches secondary Social Studies near Denver, Colorado, where he camps, hikes, fishes, and snowboards regularly.

# OTHER WORKS BY AUTHOR

### *Sloan Fitzpatrick: Middle School Journalist*

Sloan Fitzpatrick is nervous about his first day of seventh grade. His best friend moved to another state. The school bully grew taller over the summer, while Sloan remained short. Plus, he registered for a Newspaper class just because his crush was the Editor-In-Chief, even though he knew nothing about journalism. After interviewing a city politician for his first assignment, Sloan finds himself wrapped up in the school newspaper. But he also finds himself caught in a political corruption investigation and he's in way over his head. Now, how's he supposed to handle seventh grade?

o   o   o

### *In the Shadow of the Spanish Sun*

Jason embarks on a six-month journey to study abroad in Spain. When he arrives, he knows nothing but his own culture: an environment of greed, spiraling economic standards, and fast-paced rat races. After encounters with immigrant pick-up soccer, exotic cultures, and pushing the limit of fun, Jason dives too deep into these Spanish subcultures. He may find it difficult to return to his life in the United States. Then, he meets a girl. Will love turn him into an expatriate?